LADADARED BOOK⟨ NOVEL LA VIRTUAL
NOVEL, READ RED: A VIRTUAL NOVEL HYPER RED:HYPERREADLA
LA VIRALNOVEL NO   NOVEL   READ   RED,   LAVIRTUALVIRAL
NOVELALWAYSALREADYIWASALWAYSALREADYREDREADRED,ANOVEL
ABOUTOBEALLREADYREALLYREDENTIRELYVIRTUALLYREADRED,LA
VIRTUALNOVELIWASALREADYREADREADLAVIRTUALNOVELAVIRTUAL
NOVELNOVELREADRED,LAVIRALVIRGINALNOVELALWAYSAYSAL
READYIWASSALWAYSALREADYREADREADRED,ANOVELABOUTOBEALL
READYREALLYREDENTIRELYVIRTUALLYREADRED,LAVIRTUALNOVEL
IWASALREADYREADREADLAVIRTUALNOVELISALWAYSALREADSPREAD
ALREADYSPREADAVIRALALREADYVIRTUALREDVIRTUALREADLAVIR
TUALNOVELISABOUTTOBESPREADANOVELABOUTOBEALLREADYREALLY
REDENTIRELYVIRTUALLYREADBOUTTOBESPREADREDALREADYREAD
REDABOUTOBEENSPREADABOUTTOBEENTITLEDTOBEVIRTUALLALA
NOVELALREADYVIRTUALNOVELREADENTITLEDTOBEREADENTITLED
RED:REDABOUTOBEENSpRE.dLA.VIRtualhypernovel
THEREDBOOKORTHENOVELREDLAREDNONOVELLAVIRTUOSA
LALAVIRTUALUALNONOVELYESREADREDAVIRTUANONOYESNONOVEL
HYPRE.LA.VIRALRED:HYPERREDLALAVIRTUALHYPEHYPEHYPERSEX
TEXTNOVELNOVELALALREADYREADREDLALAVIRTUALVIRGINALVIRAL
REDLALAVIRTUALVIRGINALVIRALNOVELALAALWAYSALREADYIWASS
ALWAYSALREADYREADREADREDANOVELABOUTOBEALLREADYREAL
REDENTIRELYVIRTUALLYREADREDLAVIRTUALNOVELIWASALREAD
YREDVEADLAVIRTUALNOVELISALWAYSALREADSPREADALREADYSPREAD
AVIRALALREADYVIRTUALREDVIRTUALREADLAVIRTUOSANOVELIS
ABOUTTOBEALREADYREADLA.VIRTUALNOVELREALLYSPREAD
ABOUTTOBESPREADREDALREADYREDABOUTOBEREADBYIWASALREADY
REDREADLALAVIRALNOVELIWASALWAYSAM.IJANEMILYRAMJERDI
AM.IALREADSPREADALREADYSPREADAJANVIRALRAMJUNKALREADYLA
VIRTUALALAAUTHORREDVIRTUALSEXREREADLALAVIRTUALNOVELIS
ABOUTTOBESPREADABOUTTOBESPREADREDALREADYREADREDABOU
RE.LA.VIRALNOVELABOUTTOBETOBESPREADABOUREADREADLAVIR
TUALNONONOVELISALWAYSALREADSPREADALREADYSPREADREDA
LAVIRALALVIRUSSPREADABOUTTOBESPREADREDALREADYREADRED
ABOUTOBENOVELTYENSPREADABOULLALANOVELALREADYVIRTUALNO
NONONOVELREADENTITLEDTOBEAUTHOREYESREADYALREADYEN
TITLEDRED:AVIRALALREADYVIRRED,IWASALREADYREADREADBYLA
VIRTUALAUTHORNOVELINOVELTOBEABOUTOBEALLREADYREALLY
REDENTIRELYVIRTUALLYREADRED,LAVIRTUALNOVELIWASALREADY
READREADLAVIRTUALNOVELISALWAYSALREADSPREADALREADY
SPREADAVIRALALREADYVIRTUALREDVIRTUALREADLAVIRTUAL
NOVELISABOUTTOBESPREADADADADADADADALALLALADADADA
DADADA:

RE.LA.VIR

a novel by jan ramjerdi

A Black Ice Book
Normal/Tallahassee

Published by FC2 with support provided by Florida State University, the Unit
for Contemporary Literature of the Department of English at Illinois State
University, and the Illinois Arts Council

Address all inquiries to: Fiction Collective Two, Florida State University, c/o
English Department, Tallahassee, FL 32306-1580

ISBN: Paper, 1-57366-082-5

Library of Congress Cataloging-in-Publication Data

Ramjerdi, Jan.
    Re.la.vir : stories / by Jan Ramjerdi.-- 1st ed.
        p.cm.
    ISBN 1-57366-0825-5
    1. Rape--Fiction. 2. Women--Crimes against--Fiction. 3. Experimental
fiction I. Title: Re.la.vir. II. Title.

PS3568.A4455 R45 1999
813'.54--dc21

                                                    99-047452
                                                         CIP

Cover Design: Todd Michael Bushman
Book Design: Stacey Gottlieb and Owen Williams

Produced and printed in the United States of America
Printed on recycled paper with soy ink

Illinois ARTS Council
AN AGENCY OF THE STATE OF ILLINOIS

This program is
partially sponsored
by a grant from the
Illinois Arts Council

ACKNOWLEDGMENTS

I am grateful to all those who contributed to the making of **RE.LA.VIR.** I wish to thank the following individuals for their support: Larry McCaffery, Jean Vong, Beth Weatherby, Eugene Garber, Judith Johnson, Carole Maso, Amy Tan, Dennis Cooper, Ron McClean, Barbara Woloch, and my family. The following institutions gave me time and space to write the novel: California State University—Northridge, the Yaddo Foundation, the Edward Albee Foundation, the Lannon Foundation, Dorland Mountain Arts Colony, and the Woodstock Guild.

Publications Acknowledgments:
Grateful acknowledgment is made to the following publications and websites in which sections of **RE.LA.VIR** first appeared: *Black Ice, Fiction International, Two Girls Review, Quarterly West, Degenerative Prose: Writing Beyond Category* (Fiction Collective 2/Black Ice Books, eds. Amerika & Sukenick), ALT-X.com.

RE.LA.VIR
VIR.tualVisUals (VIR.VUs)
Original photographs by *Jean Vong*

**RE.LA.VIR   (RE.d
LA.VIRtualhypernovel)**

SIMulations of REd:

Mothers will make this volume
mandatory reading for their daughters.

—THE MARQUIS DE SADE

SIM1\RE.LA.VIR:
OpenMeFirst

am.i sliced

two held my legs together while another one pushed something in my bottom   yes into my rectum

    about 10 inches   i'm not sure   the handle of a jack I
think   that's what he said   the youngest one yes
that's him   in the blue jacket   Jim

    because they kept saying his name while he was doing it
while he was doing it   they kept saying Jim Jim Jim Jim Jim
Jim Jim   he didn't say anything
                                 anyway
later he said he had to fuck me   because he said they'd
bring him in anyway   the one who shaved me anyway said
 they'd bring him in   no   the driver   he said they'd bring
him in and   him   the one who shaved me   he
said they'll bring me in and beat me anyway the police the shit
out of me anyway everywhere   he shaved me everywhere
       yes   my on my head too   he shaved me but then
he saved me yes. he raped me but   but first   he shaved
 me   everywhere yes and around my bottom   yes
    no.   he said he would back out and leave the other
guys there   when he was done   yes. he did   not then
   later   they took him in and beat the
the one who shaved me   shit out of him anyway
he got me first   he was the driver no he just shaved me
then i talked a lot   back out back the car out   you
haven't done anything to me yet   by mistake   he
was trying not to the other guys were waiting outside the
car   banging Jim Jim Jim Jim Jim Jim Jim   on the hood of
the car   i just kept saying if he left now   if he left now

what i am trying to tell you is yes he raped me but then he saved me

READ ME FIRST!

Welcome to RE.dLA.VIRtualhypernovel—RE.LA.VIR®!

The following instructions on how to read RE.LA.VIR® (RiV.etSEXtinc) will help you fully experience your first VIR. tualHYP.erNONOvel. If you have questions that are not answered here, consult USE.rDOCumentation (USE.DOC) on the DOC disks: VIR.tualDICtionary (VIR.DIC.DOC), GLOss.DOC, SOURCE.DOC, NARR.EX PLIC.&TRANS.DOCs.

Technical consultants (B.E.T.T.A.SSISTS, βασσισσ) are available to assist you 24-hours, 7 days a week at 1-900-COP-AINS ($5.03 first min., $3.91 each minute thereafter).

RE.LA.VIR Features:

- TEMPLates (TEMPLs):

TEMPLs are (MACRO or micro) algorithms serving as patterns, guides, or TRANScortical path generators of alternative RE.LA.VIR MACROnarratives.

TEMPL.MACRO.MENU

- TEMPL.NARR.RAPE
- TEMPL.O!ORGAN.ON(&OFF)
- TEMPL.PANO!PTIC.on(&off)
- TEMPL.PETRO!GLYPHGRRRRRLs
- TEMPL.TOOL&DIE&TOOL&DIE&TOOL&TOOL&DIE.ME
- TEMPLE.ROMAN.CEMENt
- TEMPLE.RandOmWalk(ROWROWROWYOURBOAT)
- TEMPL.PINKGLYPHs&CLIFFs
  etc.

Each TEMPL is not only a site, it is an algorithm for how it is, or was once upon a time, constructed as a site; how you are seeing it now is how you (dear WRI.ter/reaDer) are consticting it as a TEMPLsite (as in WRI.Der SIMulations: SIM1\OpenMeFirst. SIM2\HOWRED, SIM3\cherrie, SIM4\hope, . . . , SIMn\ where n=∞) and of what and with what   in what
what

RE.aliTI.ME

Choose one now:

RE.LA.VIR.SIMuLAtions
RE.LA.VIR.STIMuLAtions
RE.LA.VIR.SIMUTiLAtions
RE.LA.VIR.STIMUTiLAtions

☞ just touch the screen

©©
Stop Depth Dive Time Dive Time Depth and Mode: Surf Hist
©©©

Welcome to: TEMPL.NARR.RAPE

Dinner.

A tureen of soup.

A green bottle with a long rectal neck.

In the foreground she leans forward her biographical elbows spread wide on the kitchen table. You see the back of her tight shaved head in semi-shadow. The angle is impossible. In the right background she is two feet spread in black Chinese sandals severed at each ankle.

"Don't move."

©©©
Stop Depth Dive Time Dive Time Depth and Mode: Surf Hist
©©©

☞ just touch the screen

Φ

porosity

what

(i, oh i

what what

don't

porosity

understand:

what

a. who or where i am
anymore); or

porosity

b. what you mean by:
porosity.)

O.K stupid, use a DIC.DOC

a what

USE A DIC.DOC

i don't know
what you mean

you
know what

what

i   mean
GOGETA DIC.DOC

what

GOGETA DIC.DOC

i mean which DIC.DOC

RE.LA.VIR.DIC.DOC!:

i   mean:

STRAP IT ON ME

NOW

porosity

SUCK IT BITCH

1pore

NOW

2pore

I

pore fungus

I just love to

por.gy

sing

pork

sing

pork barrel

this

pork belly
pork.er
pork.pie hat
por.ky
porn (porky porn i like that)
GUN
CUNT
GOT A CUNTI GOT A CUNT

song
this
song
I GOT A GUN
pork, *1* hind I GOT A
I GOT   A GUN
I GOT A GUN CUNT I
I GOT A CUNT GUN I I I

I GOT A GUN I GOT A GUN CUNT I GOT A CUNT GUN III I I I
I
I GOT A
GOT   A
CUNT GUN   I GOT A
A   CUNT GUN

foot, *2* ham, *3* I
CUNT GUN   I GOT   A
CUNT GUN I I III GOT   A   GOT
CUNTGUN   CUNTGUN

por.nog.ra.pher   one who   fatback,*4*loin CUNT
por.nog.ra.phy \-fe\ *n* [Gk *pornographos*, adj, writing *5* side, *6* Bos- GUN
   of harlots, fr. *porne* harlot + *graphein* to write; akin to   ton butt,*7* pic- CUN
   Gk *pernanai* to sell, *poros* journey-more at FARE,   nic, *8* jowl,   TGUN
   CARVE] (ca 1864) 1 : the depiction of erotic behavior   forefoot   ffffff
   (as in pictures or writing) intended to cause sexual ffss fffffssst
excitement 2: material (as in books or a photograph) that depicts erotic
   behavior   excitement — por.no.graph.ic
                         por.no.no.graph.i.cal.ly
po.ros.i.ty
                  I I I I I I I I I
                  I GOT A GUN CUNT I
                  I GOT A GUN CUNT I I
                  I GOT A CUNT GUN I I I

ff; cue

                  fffssss   fffsss

                  I I I I I I I I I
                  I GOT A I I I GOT GOT A I I   ffss ffsss
                  I GOT A I GOT A GUN CUNT I

         fffssssssssss

ff; cue!
                  I GOT A I I I I I A CUNT GUN

```
                         I A CUNT GUN
         ffssss ffss     I CUNT GUN CUNT
                         I AM A CUNT GUN
                         CUNT GUN I AM A
         ffffffsssss  ffffssss    GUN
                      fffffff     CUNT
```

FF;CUE!;FFFFFFFFFF;CU!;FF;CU!;CU;CU;FFFFF;FUC;CUE!!!

(i am thinking to)

po.ros.i.ty   -\n, *pl* -ties (14c) 1 a :   the

                                 (it's your turn now)

                    b :   the ratio of the volume of inter-
      stices (VI) of a material to the volume of its mass (VM): VI/VM 2:
PORE
por.ous   1 a:possessing or full of pores b
  : containing vessels <hardwood is ____> 2: permeable to liquids — po-
r.ous por.ous por.ous.ly — po.rous.ness yes,   poor us
poor poor us, poor all of us when you think about it   you
  think about it   you   you
BITCH!   you poor poor   you
por.phyr.ia [NL, fr. ISV *porphyrin* pss psss   ized by excretion of
excess porphyrins in the urine   ppppssss   psssssssss psss
(open your eyes bitch   LOOK AT ME WHEN I SHOWER YOU
W/ < > you you BITCH!) (i hope you will not tell on me) and by
extreme sensitivity to light
por.phy.rin   n [ISV, fr. Gk *porphyrin*   purple](1910): any of
  various VIRulent agents with a VIRtual   (VIR.VIR) structure that
consists essentially of   wettings&
  four pyrrole rings   weddings
      pyrrole [fr. G *pyrrhotes* redness; fr. *pyrrhos* red, fr. *pyr* fire—
          more at FIRE] (1835)   rings TEMPL:ROMAN.CEMENt
          heavy losses in defeating the Romans](1885): a victory
          won at exces- Pyr.rhic *Pyrrhus*, king of *Pyrrhon*   here
kitty kitty kitty prrrr prrrr Pyrrho, 4th cent. B. C. Gk. philosopher](ca.ca
1670) 1: the doctrines of
      sive cost   joined by four = C- groups   ; *esp* : (as
  chlorophyll   or
  hemoglobin) containing a central metal: atom and usu.
exhibiting bio-

logical activity.

STOP
STOP

DS;DS   that doesn't work any more
                               Little Red Dead Leaf: LITTLE Dead Red
DIC!   I   TOLD   YOU   TO   GO   GET
RE>LA>VIR>DIC>DOC NOT WEB>DIC>DOC BITCH!

IF YOU WANT TO QUIT DIC.DOC   SET DIC.DOC = OFF
                    OK: take that stupid LITTLE O!rgan OFF
SET O!O!rgan=OFF

SET O!O!RGANON=OFF   need a buzz saw to

z   zzzz zZZZZZZZzz ZZZZZZ zzzZZZZZZzzzzz   ZZZZZZzz

☞ just touch the screen
                          ▲   SOURCE.DOC
                    WEB.ster's   Nth New
                                             Collegiate
                                             DIC.tionary

SET DIC=OFF
SET DIC=OFF!
å ✉ ⊃——— k ><? ≅ ≅ ==   =O ?
ΦΦ   OFF   A Μερριαμ–Ωεβστερ ®

                               MERRIAM-WEBSTER INC., Publishers
☞ just touch the screen

                          Φ

                     TEMPLate

                   po.ros.i.ty

dear, abcdefg ABCDEF   what   happens then

symbol
αβχδεφγ ΑΒΧΔΕΦ
lc: 14 16 18 24
ϕ ϕ ϕ Φ
uc
ΦΦΦΦ Imagine a little red leaf upon a shore any where
there is an ocean still and a wish for a stable season:

Springfield, Massachusetts, U.S.A
Copy(right!) by Merriam-Webster Inc. 2009

abcdefg ABCDEF

symbol   GRRRRRR SET DIC = OFF!
αβχδεφγ ΑΒΧΔΕΦ
lc: 14 16 18 24

        i told you
☞   just touch the screen TAKE THAT STUPID

BODY/   :ORGAN.OFF
TEMPL   :ORGAN.ON   .OFF
  .ON   .OFF NOW IT'S YOUR YOUR TURN   BEND
OVER   I GOT A GUN   SO BEND OVER AND SPREAD

                      queenie   YOU BITCH!

po.ros.i.ty   (oh, hi Ivan)
                you know the One   the Terrible
                      ΦI.van

TEMPLate:
; how you are seeing it is how you are yourself constructing it
now BODY/
now TEMPL: for example:

                      SIM\2: RE.LA.VIR
O!ORGAN.ON   .OFF   HOWRED.RE.LA.VIR
                      HOWIRED.RE.LA.VIR
.DIC   or.ga.non n   [Gk, lit.tool —:an instrument for acquiring
        more at ORGAN](1543)   knowledge
                      cherrie.re.la.vir

SET ORGAN = OFF   good girl,
                              hope

now you are constructing it REAL.TI.ME as a TEMPLsitewithin
each WRIter.REaDerSIMulation of REd.LA.VIRtualhypernonono
vel, or RE.LA.VIR for short.

Each NARR.ativeTEMPLate (NARR.TEMPL) which restores the
primacy of the fixed model of the form involves the opposite
of squaring, roadways, and bridges (as in stone-carving hope—
simply:

        i told you
                            FIXLOCAT:LEAF

☞ justtouch the screen   ▲
                                      - -

        Imagine a little red leaf upon a scene any where there
is an ocean still and a wish for a stable season.

Imagine a little red leaf

{some interface.}

> She's cute—the other one.
> She has a cute cunt.
> I'm already thinking about fucking her when I see her sitting at a table in the health food store. She follows us to an outside table. Says she's staying with friends of her girlfriend who are not there, her luggage locked inside the condo. She doesn't know them. There's no one home, no note, no key. She's worried about ending up in some motel. I would like to fuck her. She's asking for it. Chain smoking Camels talking about wanting to be a writer. I'd like to fuck her up the ass. I have the tools. She has the holes.
> "It sounds like you're living such an exciting life."
> "Is there a sequel?"
> "What time is it? Could you tell me?"
> He stuffs his penis in her mouth. And knows there is a white form that fits him now he is in command of all the pain. He pushes her head down hard and holds it there says yeah yeah yeah choke on it bitch as if it were so simple the attachment of these two classes: raped and rapist.
> "Yeah, right where the danger is, grows what rescue as well."
> "Choke on it."
> She's got to swallow it. Her mouth is a place where things turn into what they are:

Also the word _____.

{exit interface}

the only <u>truth</u> in this <u>story</u> is what they do to your <u>body</u>

rape: for a while i identify with this : <u>truth</u> <u>story</u> <u>body</u>
rape: for a while <u>i</u> <u>identify</u> with what they do to my <u>truth</u> <u>story</u> <u>body</u> <u>body</u>.

Rape.	He enamels her hands.
Rape.	With or without windows.
Rape.	She was inherited.
Rape.	Is our allowance,
Rape.	It is a diagram.
Rape.	

There is difficulty in recapturing the word.
Listen.

Rape.	Read rape.
Consider.	Rape.
Rape.	Out loud.
Rape.	Are you familiar with her colon.

STOP

☞ just touch the screen

(index or fist)

To access TEMPLs:

1. Clear screen by pressing the WhiteButton; TEMPL.ateMACRO.ME.NU will appear on your screen.

2. Choose TEMPLate by double clicking mouse on the selected box in TEMPL.ateMACRO.ME.NU (or just touch the screen).

3. TEMPL.atemicroME.NU will then appear on your screen. Select subTEMPLate by double clicking mouse on chosen option, or (you got it) just touch the screen.

If your keyboard does not have the WhiteButton, see your manual for further instructions on how to obtain a TRANSLAtor key from your local RiV.etSEX.tinc (RV.SEX) dealer.

- SCREE.nalREALities: VIR.tualVisUals (VIR.VUs) & VIR.tualVidEOs (VIR.VEOs)

If you are equipped with a color monitor and a video port please press CTRL and XVID (SIMultaneously) now.

XVID   SIM now

You will see a REd screen initially. Watch for more than REd.

In approximately 45 seconds your retinas will adjust.

Now you should see letters in ASS.embleME.MAI.1ME language (ASS.ME.MAI.ME)which specify ALT.ernativeSCREE.nalREALities (ALT.SCREE.REALs) you may choose to translate into VIR.VUs and/or VIR.VEOs on your screen by highlighting a selection of the text and clicking twice.

(Remember, watch for more than REd.)

SIMSIM   SIMSIM

A.M.I.ME/A.M.I.ME/A.M.I.ME/A.M.I.///ME//A.M.I.M.E.//ME//
A.M.I.ME/A.M.I.ME/A.M.I.ME//ALT.RE.AL::/A.M.I.ME//A.M.I.//
ME//A.M.I.ME/A.M.I.ME//ALT.REAL::/A.M.I.ME//A.M.M.I.ME//
A.M.I.ME//A.M.I./ALT.RE.AL//ME//A.M.I.ME/A.M.I.alt.re.al.me/
ME//A.M.I./ME//A./M.I./ME//A.M.I./ME//A.M.M.I.ME/
A.M.I.ME/AM.I.ME?/ALT.RE.AL::E///A.M.I.//ME//A.M.I.ME//
A.M.I.ME//A.M.I.ME//A.M.I.ME//A.M.I.ME//A.M.M.I.ME//
A.M.I.ME//A.M.I.ME//A.M.I.ME//A.M.I.//ALTREAL:://ME//
A.M.I.ME//A.M.I.ME//A.M.I.ME//A.M.M.I.ME//A.M.I.//ME//
ALT.RE.AL.E::EE::EPISTOL:://A.M.I./EE.EPISTOL.//ME//A.M.I.ME/
/A.M.I.ME//A.M.I./ME//PISTOL//ME//A.M.I.ME//AM.I//
ALTREAL:EPISTOL:://ME/A.M.I.ME//A.M.M.I.ME//A.M.I.ME//
A.M.I.ME/ALTREAL:EPISTOL:://ME//A.M.I.ME//A.M.I.ME//
A.M.I.ME//A.M.I.ME//A.M.I.ME//A.M.M.I.ME//E.PIST//RE.//AL/
E./PIST//RE.//AL/PIST//RE.AL//PIST//I//AM.I/RE./PIST/AL/RE.

¶¶¶¶¶¶¶¶¶¶¶7¶¶¶¶¶¶¶¶¶¶¶¶¶¶¶¶¶¶¶¶¶¶7X¶¶¶
¶¶¶¶¶¶¶¶¶¶¶¶¶¶¶¶¶¶¶¶¶¶¶¶¶¶¶¶¶¶¶¶
¶¶¶¶¶¶¶¶¶¶¶¶¶¶¶¶¶¶¶¶¶¶¶7777XXX¶¶¶¶

ALT.REAL::REAL.E.PISTOL::☞IGOTAGUN.IGOTACUNTGUNIGOTAG
UN.IGOTACUNTGUNIGOTAGUN.IGOTACUNTGUNIGOTAGUN.IGOT
ACUNTGUN

DEARA.M.I.QUE:N.I(A)FA(I)CONOL.C.C.VIR.VEO.4.U@NATUR.ALLY
@LA@LA@CA.CA.N.U.COM@22B&B&CC@TI.ME::6:09A.M.I.ME.

JUST LEAVE ME ALONE
JUST LEAVE ME
ALOWWWWWWN
JUST LEAVE ME
ALOWWWN LET ME BE
JUST LET ME JUST
LET ME JUST LET ME BE!

AR: Yes, Monthly, Private: A shaving house, AC, little wood
cuts, a little aqua door to, two china bowls of white rice, a
pair of long-necked cranes, their line of flight, her paper
screens, nearly the last and best regular window, raindrops, a
pink cliff between the curtains, easy easy express, pink glyphs,
a pot of green tea, a waterfall, best wet, waves and waves of,
bye bye The Land of Perfect Bliss, all to be no no no, yes, yes
yes, we had a good last summer there, palm trees, didn't we,
no, pine trees, passing and passing balloons, your tight red,
your little tight red leaf, cut up, cunt up, and don't forget, my
ankle chains, cuffs and clams, temple of mud and torn ribbons, temple of raindrops, you and your body rips, thumbcuff,
why is there that scissor between, choked between, having
choked on, a pink razor, so die, little red cunt, cunt i let
leave, it is so natural to miss you like this, little red leaf, our
little shaving house, house and house cunts and cunts and
cunt you cunt you and cut you, cut you and bless you, fuck
you and bless you who have taken who have you taken to
shaving you now who shaves you now who shaves the dead, so

polite in the front, not nearly so behind, a little beneath, then lower, lower, down on your knees, down on your hands and knees, bend over

dead
who fucks
the dead.

cut up, cunt up, and don't forget my ankle chains, cuffs you and your body rips, that scissor between choked choked on cunt you cunt you cut you fuck you in the front behind down on your hands and knees, bend over and dead

Welcome to You: The Woman Who Was NARRaped

⬚ TEMPL.NARR.RAPEmicroME.
NU

Welcome to You: The Woman Who Was NAR.Raped!

SHOW.ME TI.ME   01:1901

It's SHOW&TELL TI.ME girls & boys!

SHOW&TELL&SHOW&TELL&SHOW&SHOW&TELLTI.METELLTE
LL&TI.MEWHATDIDTHEYWHATDIDTOYOURBODYGIRL GRRRRRR
GRRR
GRRRRRRRLLLLLLL
SHOW&TELL&SHOW   DONTTELLSHOW&SHOW&SHOW

VIR.VEO.ME.
NU

  FUCKED TIL SHE
  I'M NOT THE SAME
  I FEEL NO PAIN
  THIS ACTION AND REACTION GOES ON AND ON
  SHE WON'T CRY ANYMORE
  I REMOVE HER BUTTPLUG
  postromoanalpost: it keeps me erect
                       from falling on all fours
                       it's an extension of my body

spine, it
i can attach myself to
                      the ground the ground with it

    every i i can buttfuck

            every i i i   can
               under 8 thin robes of dark
               red wore glossed silk when i
i went to the Palac   e i wore a d
ark crimson rubb   er appliance
to assfuck glos glos glos   sed silk i want to 8

over eight

                    thin knots under robes of dark red
                    8 knots of drk rd slk glos glos 8 &
8 glos gls & sht 8 8 gls & sht eight knts slk & sht slk & sht gls
gls sht gls 8 & 8 sht 8 sht 8 & 8sht8sht8sht8&8sht sht8&8sh8sh
t

SELECT SPEED OPTION SSO: $S(t) = S(t-1)^{**(1/ß)}$

               where:

                    $S(t)$ = Speed in time t
                    $S(t-1)$ = Speed in time t-1
                    $ß>0$ = Fixed unknown parameter

     Let ß =
              8 glos pls & sht 8 8 pls & sht eight knts slk
& sht slk & sht pls pls sht pls 8 & 8 sht 8 sht 8 &
        8sht8sht8sht8&8sht sht8&8sh8shshshshshshsh
t

justgotojustgotojustgotosleeeepjus   o
tojustotojustotosleepjustgotojustgotojustgotosleepjustotojustoto
justotosleepjustotosleeeeee   eee   pppp eee   pee   o
    pee pee   (i hope you will not tell
on me)

RE.VOLVE.HER>>RE.VULVE.HER>>RE.VALVE.HER>>RE.VIRVE.HER>
>FUCK>>FUCK>>HER>>HERE IS WHERE I FUCK HERRE.
VIRV>>HER>>FUCK>>IN>>RE.VOLVE.HER>>NOW>>IT'S>>YOUR
>>TURN>>NOW>>RE.VIRV>>RE.VIRV>>RRR>>RRRRR>>RE>>RE>>
RE>>VERT>>RE>>LA>>>VIRT

     i feel no pain

                    i'm not the same

                    I'M ALREADY DEAD
     I'M ALREADY DEADI'M ALREADY DEAD I'M ALREADY
DEAD I'M ALREADY DEAD   I'M ALREADY DEAD

she has replaced me

I'M ALREADY DEAD   I'M ALREADY DEAD I'M   ALREADY
DEAD I'M ALREADY DEAD   I'M ALREADY DEAD   I'M
ALREADY DEADDEAD I'M ALREADY DEADRED I'M ALREADY
DEAD
ff;cue
FFFKYOU

<<RE.VOLVE.HER>>

they help me get up on the examination table, i can't sit, i crawl, then flop down on my side, they roll me on to my back, we're going to lift your feet into the stirrips, can you scoot down, the light between my legs. A female nurse positions the light a young male policeman with a crewcut takes notes. The doctor has hairy hands i watch him put on a latex glove then another the hair still shows beneath the latex. i feel a wide tube slide up my vagina I think a turkey baster suck it all out sperm, engine oil, antifreeze. then they stick one up my ass, i scream, the nurse holds my hand, it's ok, it'll be over soon, her hand is so cold.

a man with a camera, yes, a cameraman, comes in to take pictures while the doctor examines me; between my legs

front shot bloody cunt flash flash the doctor spreads it open and speaks into a microcassette, contusion, wrench, laceration, they shaved me, laceration, with a single-edged razor, laceration, contusion, tire jack, burn, cigarette lighter, burn, battery acid, the nurse looks sympathetic, the cameraman comes closer flash flash, get this also, close-up cigarette burns inner right thigh from knee to clitoris, burn, lighter, laceration, broken bottle, flash flash;

and back, can you scoot down more, the doctor says, a little more, the nurse raises the stirrups higher, just relax, just relax, just relax the doctor says and spreads my cheeks sticks a latex finger in my damaged rectum, I try to just take it, just take it, just take it, whatever, one more thing up my ass, whatever, i'm alive, he says do you know what this green fluid is? antifreeze, whatever, flash flash flash-flash flash;

HOWIRED.RE.LA.VIR

VIR.VEO.ME.NU: ☐ HOW.RE.dLA.VIR RE.asSEMBLES PLOT
PLOT&PLOT&PLOT__|___|___|___|___|___|___|___|___|___|___|
___|___|___|___|___|___|_____|___|___|___|___|___|___|___|__|__
_|___|___|___|___|___|_____|___|___|_____
_____|___|___|_____

```
_I___I___I___I___I___I___I___I___I___I___I___I___I___I___I__
_I_____I___I___I___I___I___I___I___I___I___I___I___I___I___I
___I___I_____I___I___I___I___I___I___I___I___I___I___I___I__
_____cumplot_____cumplot
_I___I___I_____I__
_I_____
___I___I_____
_____I___I_____
_____I___I_____
_____I___I_____
_____I___I_____
_____cumplot___
__cumplot_____cumplot_____
_____
cumplot___I___I___I___I___I_____I___I___I_____
_____I___I___I___I_____HOWIRED.RE.LA.VIR_____
_____I___I___I_____A___NOVEL_____
_____I___I_____WR.IDe_____BY___
_____I___I_____howred__a__acton
_____I___I_____
_____I___I_____
_____I___I___
```

[NARR.EXPLIC.&TRANS.DOC

: <u>CUM.PLOT</u>: where all stories are the result of [FUCK! FUCK
PLOT!] plotting, and plotting and very much machination:

I.VAN a man within a machine within a machine within a ma-
chine with in a machine in a machine in a machine SHOVE IT IN IN in
a machine FUCK ME IN IN FUCK me in a machine with in in
with in a machine in in IN FUCK IN HARD IT a machine FUCK
ME FUCK ME UP IT UP MY BUTT WITH IT A MACHINE SHOVE IT
IN IN A MACHINE AND UP UP AND IN IN AND UP IN A MACHINE
MACHINATE ME IN A MACHINE IMAGINATE ME IMAGINE ATE
ME IN A MACHINE IN A MACHINE IMAGINE ME ATE ME IN A
MACHINE ATE ME SPLAY ME HATE ME RAPE ME IN A MACHINE
IN A MACHINE IN A MACHINE IN A MACHINE IN A MACHI SHE
she she IN A MACHI I. shI. shI.I shI. I. I.   I. I.I. I.I. I.I. I.
                    I. I.I. I.I. I.I. I.I. I. I.
                    I. I.   I. I.I. I.I. I.I. I.
                    oh hi   I.VAN

                         ΦI.VAN]

[NARR.EXPLIC.&TRANS.DOC]

SET NARR.EXPLIC.&TRANS.DOC = OFF

If this is what you want this is what you get if this is what

you want this is what you get if this is what you want this is
what you get this is what you get this is what you get this is
what want you want get what you want want if this is what
you want this is what you get get what you get what you get
this is what you want this is what you get what you want get
want get want this is what you want this is what you get this
is what you want this is what you get [repeat 7X]

TEMPL.NARR.RAPEmicroME.
NU

just touch the screen
☞

    ☐ Splash!

    ☐ then count and count

    ☐ one thousand one one thousand two one one one thous and

    ☐ recount

    ☐ one one thousand two

    ☐ as he severs the sinews above your heels

breasts, may I? I lift my head, the nurse unties the tie at the
back of my neck, the doctor pulls the paper down to just below my right breast, did they do this to you with a razor too?
no, jumper cables, I can feel the cameraman's breath on me
when he does a closeup of where the nipple was; the nurse
covers my breast and the doctor pulls the paper down around
the left one; they didn't hurt this one, I say, it looks a little
bruised he says, and the cameraman shoots the breast from
two angles flash flash;

the doctor asks if he can pull down the sheet that is over my
legs to see my belly; i say yes; he pulls the sheet down and
lifts the lower part of the gown, the top falls open too, he
closes it, he squeezes my internal organs, I feel it all the way
from cunt to rectum to neck, does it hurt, hurt yes, down
around my neck, up my rectum to my throat; I taste blood,
shit, semen, antifreeze, engine oil, all that coming in my mouth;
i turn my head; i vomit on the paper sheet, blood shit semen
antifreeze engine oil the nurse wipes my mouth and cheek,
scoops my vomit into a jar, covers the rest with a paper sheet,
gives me a little paper cup of warm warm water

can you sit up, the doctor says

i try

should i be videotaping this, the cameraman asks

no, i can't, it feels like i've swallowed a knife anally, blood and slime and something hard slide out my rectum onto the paper sheet, part of my spinal column, a glob of some body part, my liver i think i'm stuck to it

it hangs out my rectum

flash flash flash

the doctor helps the cameraman insert a 60" swivel head FlexCam up my butt. (It's 18" flexible gooseneck offers precise camera positioning—easily, quickly, flexible.)

can you take it out

we need to document everything before we can begin treatment

ok, lift your head up so i can see the back of your neck,

what's this from

i forget, oh yeah they had dog chains, and leashes

he takes my hand spreads it open on the paper sheet

◻ now it's your turn to enter MACRO.TEMPL.NARR.RAPE!

Welcome to TEMPL.NARR.RAPE!

You have just entered TEMPL.NARR.RAPE.

To establish your location in<_____>RE.LA.VIR's <enter current version name> TEMPL.NARR.RAPE just touch the screen

☞HOW.RED.

▲

FIXLOCAT:CUNT

☞WI.RED

Clamps: You become anonymous then when he shaves
           you with ankle chains, a metal collar, and he
nipple clamps you; he photographs you, spreads you with a nine-
       inch spoon; he inserts   potatoes, rhinestones, raw
meat, a   beer bottle,
       drink up honey, I've got money,and   he spends you
quarters you link by link from anus to armpit   from from
                                                cunt   to
cerebellum   he bank notes you bank notes and
cranks you.

Ha! Ha! There's no conflict between us now!

STOP

       why am i so seen

                   ☐ dead and spread

                   ☐ cut up   cunt up

                   ☐ dead and dead by

STOP
Invalid Command
STOP
Invalid Command

                   ☐ dead and spread

                   ☐ cut up   cunt up

                   ☐ dead and dead by

                   ☐ you: the woman who is raped

                   ☐ you: the man who is made to rape

□ you: rape: you

He plays back the video while he narrates your disorganized body splay on the pavement.

Here is a severed leg.

Here is half a head.

Here is the brick on the temple that means 'I love you.'

_____

VIR.VEO: □ dead and dead by
VIRtualVidEO:

_____

SIMSIMSIMSTIMSIMISITHIMSTIMHIMSIMHIMSTIMSTIMSIMHIMSIM

This is not really real   ly   happening
SIM HIM   SIM STIM

He plays back the video while he narrates your disorganized body splay on the pavement.

Here is a severed leg.

Here is half a head.

Here is the brick on the temple that means 'I love
you.'

this is not really happening

Here is the brick on the temple that means 'I love
you.'

Here is half a head.

Here is a severed leg.

He plays back the video while he narrates your disorganized body splay on the pavement.

ffffff;cue   this is not real thisisnotreal
thisisnotreal ly hap pen   isnotreal
in   in ing   ThisisnotREalthis thisis thisisnotREal
thisisnotRE al LLLYhapp en   ing A.M.I.   hap penenen

ing to ME   lyME/A.M.I.ME// A.M.I. ME/A.M.I.///ME/
/A.M.M.I.//ME//A.M.I.ME/A.M.I.ME/A.M.I.ME/ ALT.RE.AL::/A.M.I.ME/
/A.M.I.//ME//A.M.I.MEA.M.I.ME//ALT.RE
AL::/A.M.I.ME//A.M.M.I.ME//A.M.I.ME//A.M.I./ALT.RE.AL//ME//
A.M.I.ME/A.M.I.alt.re.al.me/ME// YOU BET YOUR LIFE YOU
        YOU BET YOUR LIFE   IT
                                 SH   IT IS

Look. This is thrilling!

Here is where I rip her open from the the back of her neck and remove her spine.

Here is where I introduce my tool to her bowel.

it takes a long time

i use WD-40 and the wedge-one wand from RE.LA.VIR's

οβολUTILItyBOx:

☐ It is a five-and-a-half foot length of stout aluminum pipe—holes drilled in the end—soldered to a device of short, bendable steel rods. It looks, very roughly, like a hand with crooked and spread fingers, the middle finger long, upright, and sharpened into a cutting tool.

Here is a plastic bag I caught in the branch of a tree.

Here's a spleen.

Here is where I tear the nipple off her chest.

Here is where I make her breathe into the plastic bag so she won't faint.

Here is where she begs and begs and begs and begs.

Here's a woman passing by, she says, oh, it's just the bag removal guy.

And so the plot goes: here is your colon on display, here is your liver, here is your heart.

Look! It's still throbbing.

Now you are the photographed and videoed really real this is really happening and so, so narrated:

I do not know the woman I am until I am raped.

I do not know the woman I am until I am raped.

I do not know the woman
I am until I am raped

[repeat 7X] ☐ so read and read and read by

☐ so dead and dead by

☐ so dead and dead by

STOP!

Invalid Command

HELP

**To EXIT TEMPL.NARR.RAPE TYPE AN X

X

TO RETURN TO RE.LA.VIR MAIN MENU TYPE AN H
TO RETURN TO READMEFIRST TYPE A D

H

_____

RE.LA.VIR MAIN MENU

_____

☐ Edit
☐ Park
☐ Insert
☐ He
☐ Go to . . .
☐ Toolbox
☐ Windows
☐ To return to . . .
☐ She
☐ Help balloons

      ☐ He
☐ WRI.RE.AVE

_____

                    ☐ Park

SELECT PARK MODE=   PASSF: PASSIVE FORGETTING
                     ACTF: ACTIVE FORGETTING

PASSF

PASSFmicroME.NU

    ☐ I (Heart) MINIGOLF

    ☐ JUSTGOTOSLEEPJUSTO!TOSLEEP

    ☐ ABOATTOBALI

    ☐ THE19THCENT&ME

    ☐ METALCUNT

    ☐ EVERYBODYSMILENOW

Welcome to THE19THCENT&ME!

HA! HA!

Someone finishes the job after your death.

D
D;D;D

RE.VOLVE.HER>>RE.VULVE.HER>>RE.VALVE.HER>>RE.VIRVE.HER>
>FUCK>>FUCK>>HER>>HERE IS WHERE I FUCK HER
RE.VIRV>>HER>>FUCK>>IN>>RE.VOLVE.HER>>NOW>>IT'S>>YOUR
>>TURN>>NOW>>RE.VIRV>>RE.VIRV>>RRR>>RRRRR>>RE>>RE>>
RE>>VERT>>RE>>LA>>>VIRT

       i feel no pain

       i'm not the same
ff;cue

    I grab a pussy stick. Smooth driftwood. It's about four inches around and two feet long with a fork at the end. I picked it up earlier when i was walking down the beach. And I shove it in her—dry.
    She screams.
    No one can hear you.
    Make all the noise you want BITCH.
    I scream too. BITCH. ASS CUNT. TAKE IT UP THE ASS

CUNT QUEENIE LIKE YOU DID TO ME. FUCK ME UP THE ASS LIKE YOU LIKE IT FEELS GOOD DOES IT DOES IT FEEL GOOD R E A L GOOD GOOEY LIKE IT LIKE IT GOOD FEEL ME UP YOURS UP YOURS UP YOUR FUCKING BUTT UP YOUR FUCKING FUCKING BUTTFUCKER BUTTFUCKER BUTTFUCKING BITCH YEAH THAT'S RIGHT BITCH BUTTFUCKER BITCH I'M GONNA FUCK YOUR FUCKING ASS CUNT BITCH YEAH SCREAM BITCH SCREAM ALL YOU FUCKING WANT BITCH I'M GONNA FFFFUCK YOU AND FFFFUCK YOU BUTTTT   FFFFFFUCK YOU BUTTTTFFFFFUCK BUTTFFUCKER BUTTTFUC KK KKKK KK

 YEAH TAKE IT BITCH CREAM YOU UP THE BUTT TIL YOU SPILL AND SPILL IT ALL BITCH SPILL IT ALL YOUR SHIT ALL YOUR SHIT ALL OVER YOUR WHITE BLOODY SHITTY ASS CUNT

 I pull the stick out. It's all covered with shit. I wipe it off with my fingers, taste it, then smear it all over her lips.
 I pick up an old burnt log. It's big. I shove it up her ass. It takes two hands. I grab it between my legs and ride it up and down. I stick my fingers in her mouth, bridle her.
 I split the sides of her mouth when I come in screams and gobs and gobs and streams of urine and feces, and who knows what else, blood, something gooey.
 She hasn't come yet.
 Just kill me. I don't care.
 Fuck you.
 I grab the seaweed all covered with sand and shove it down her throat. I keep pushing until I'm in up to my elbow. I fist fuck her throat.
 I squat over her and release the rest of the feces and urine left in me.
 She lies there on her stomach quietly.
 The burnt end of the log sticks straight out her ass. I yank it out. She doesn't move.
 Roll over.
 She doesn't.
 ROLL OVER.
 She doesn't.
 I roll her over. Her breasts are torn. Sand sticks to the blood. There's more blood and sand on her belly and a few gobs of shit. I spread her legs open and shove the burnt end of the log up her cunt. The shitty end hangs out between her legs. I smear shit on her belly. Write my name in it.

 Then I walk away.
 DIE. FUCKING BITCH.

 There, she's dead now.
 I fucked her dead cunt until she died.

The big vein in my leg is pounding. I have lost my clothes. I walk along the path. Leave the path. Walk naked into the Montauk woods. I am the naked natural woman who rapes, is raped. I do not know the woman i am until i am raped. I do not know the woman i am until i rape the woman i am   queenie she's dead   now   electronic   i can be myself   neon pink metallic fiberglass &glazed   i   am   the   rapist wrapped in a woman's body weapons&tools i am the body in rapist who has aborted every body organ
buried in jars of   formaldehyde   I bury every jar of you queenie bury you in the yard of the _____ Prison for Female Rapists   Body Parts   & yet heave ho! i am still alive   i'm still alive   & raping queenie. i return to you   within a hundred viewing jars unearthed from the: TEMPL.MACRO:PRISONYARD.

I label each:

Jar   1:   I squeeze her colon to express her self. Title1:
                        Turbulent Movemnt
Jar   2:   practical aspirations: i squeeze her ovaries
Jar   3.   Its heart was in the right place.
                              Heart on a RR spike
Jar   4..   Assumption of the VIRginQUEenie: parallel lam
                        anal layers EXT INT
Jar   5.   I fill her rectum with rocks: CUNT, flesh, sand
                        ALTer   NET
            slice it at the sigmoid & tie it shut w/ layers

pliers   web   i inspect her anus
residents   body is rotated
meat   segmented, immobile, frozen space.
fishrest, bend   house with pulleys & baskets;   iron
herbs   who can be left to die   spikes
dead   sea grass bows
clean   Title: following 2 paths   *Logos*

Jar   6.   I cut off my middle finger at the joint closest to my hand. I do it on her breast, the blood spills down her neck. i cut off her breast too & her bowel I roll her over and yank out a foot of her intestine. and cut it off. I wrap the colon around my finger and tie it like a bow. I put it in a middle-sized jar and write:
        rest, bend

Jar   7.   I roll her over again, her pubic hair is dark and curly. I comb it, wet it, wet it wet it. then i shave it closely, crying, crying.

i miss you little queenie.

I gather all i can into a little jar i add some pretty little stones and sea water. i label it in tiny letters:

so much resignation   there is no such thinga collection
no name is signed   lost 11/19/93

i do many vile things to her pussy—from one corpse to another—i fuck her in every way i can think of including propped up on a big log i lug her over to and arrange her so that my ass touches her open cunt when i'm down on my hands and knees fucking myself in the butt watching the sea, the burnt end of the log shoved up into her uterus so it stays tight. I rip my rectum getting it in. i scream and cry.

A ship passes by.

I bungie cord her to the biggest log I can find. I pretend i am a wild animal and i scavenge her. i pretend i am a crow and i peck at her eyes.

i stop & eat the bread and wine we brought for a picnic lunch.

She's a part now.

Jar
8.   her head: i open her mouth. run my index finger over
        each tooth, the space between her cheeks and her gums,
        beneath her upper lip and her gums, between her lower lip
        and her gums. then i put my finger in my cunt and back to
        her gums again. i do this until i am about to come. then i
straddle her head. pull her tongue out, it's still warm and press it from
my clit to my anus clit to anus clit to clit clit   a   ship
passes   shove two fingers through near the tip   her tongue it's
still warm and bleeds   anus   shove my finger through her tongue
there is the sound of a ship's horn   up my anus to
anus to   anus anus i
squat   into   when i'm about to come i pull out her tongue
down   i hold her tongue against my
on   & ejaculate gobs
face   breasts   into her open
mouth   Then i rinse her mouth out with sand and
and ride her   seaweed. i fill a wine bottle with sea water
head like a beach & pour it down her throat. it all comes out
ball back & forth her severed neck on the sand. i push a
back & forth   fingertip in the corner of her eye and pop it i
press my   out. I do the same to the other one. I slip

hands against her them one at a time slowly up my cunt
ears to keep her to keep them there for a while days maybe
head still. always so i won't forget her body, head
I put her down on the sand and lie down
beside her I pull her to me. roll her head
closer. press my breasts into hers. I wish
she could look at me now. I squeeze my cunt
muscles and lick the bleeding holes where her eyes were she still
bleeds.

       i haven't anything strong enough to sever
bones. i try strapping her to the big log and pulling on her arm
as hard as i can to pop the socket a little but the flesh won't
tear. I hack around her shoulder and armpit with my Swiss
Army knife and sever some muscles and tendons. and try again.
after a few more tries it comes apart. I sit on the sand and
cradle her cute little arm. I smooth her arm hairs, suck each
fingertip, she likes that, i fold the fingers into a fist and rub
my cunt, slide it back and forth a little & try to ram her up my
ass. it doesn't work because her wrist keeps bending so i hold
her middle two fingers up and push them into my ass. i do it
lying on my back knees bent back ass pointed up to the blue
blue sky.

    I live through this.
but she, of course, does not.

I live through this.
but she, of course, does not.

TYPE AN H

H

There's no place like ____.
There's no place like ____.
There's no place like ____.
[click heels & repeat 7X]

Note: Simultaneous on-line WRI.Ding of RE.LA.VIR requires
RV.SEXtinc twisted sister cables X0T1CA and corresponding
ports.

> should i listen to the
> voices in my head
>
> (i hope you won't

tell on me.)

$$$$$$$$$Registering Ownership: RiV.etSpeak (RV.S)$$$$$$$$$$

When you open RE.LA.VIR, it will appear as an independent, if
interconnected, document in its own right. If you purchased
RE.LA.VIR in hard-copy form, you will notice that unlike a
fully ACTualized (vs. VIRtualized) hypertext system, RE.LA.VIR
is a *Physical Book*, offering the WRI.ter/reaDer (WRI.Der) a
REAL.TI.ME SIMulation of the InterActive Electronic Text-Pro-
cessing Environment (I.AET.PE) that produced this printed
DOCU.version of RE.LA.VIR (*PB*.DOCU.RE.LA.VIR).

If you are an electronic WRI.Der of RE.LA.VIR, you will be
prompted by RiV.etSpeak to register your version of RE.LA.VIR
by naming it. There is a $79 charge for registering RE.LA.VIR:
please snail mail to: Jan Ramjerdi@CSUN-ENGDept//18111
NordhoffSt//91330 or e-money::jrpriggybank^962500179::200
11:1675*20115/5289@ARRG{H: H.H}

Your version will include all changes you have made to
RE.LA.VIR as you WRI.De your own narrative path through
RE.LA.VIR's TEMPLates. All your choices—textual, visual, au-
ral—made from RE.LA.VIR's MACRO and microME.NUs, VIR.VU
and VIR.VEO prompts, as well as any changes and additions
you have made yourself: corrections, comments (spoken or
written), recorders, photo images, MEMO.REX, a small foot-
print overwrites (WRI.tesRE.ads&sAVEs—WRI.RE.AVEs) as you
WRI.De RE.LA.VIR.

The original will be retained only if you make a copy of it, as, for example, MY.RE.LA.VIR and then WRI.teREad&sAVE:

WRI.RE.AVE {MY.}RE.LA.VIR

on your registered copy of RE.LA.VIR, named as:

optional
{yourname(mo/date/yr)}.RE.LA.VIR

PLS ENTER YOUR NAME (and DATE) NOW:

_____(   )

Hello, <u>yourname</u>.

Today is <u>today's date</u>.

Welcome to <u>yourname</u>.RE.LA.VIR—your personal version of RE.LA.VIR!

Your version will be added to the collective version, CO.RE.LA.VIR, available on WWW through accessing RiV.etSpeak (RV.S) :

☞ Just speak RiV.etHEAD!

▲

FIXLOCAT:iuuq://www.rvsex.tinc/igmsdoodoo/spk

✌

HI igmsdoodoo/spk

On-line RE.LA.VIR WRI.Ders will be able to access your version in whole or in part by selecting the ownership name you have specified, followed by .RE.LA.VIR.

WRI.Der   Version name

Examples: cherrie   HOWRED.RE.LA.VIR
               HOWRED   cherrie.re.la.vir
               i   HOWIREd.RE.LA.VIR
               CUNT   WI.REd.RE.LA.VIR
               HOWIRED   igmsdoodoo/spk.RE.LA.VIR
               HOWIRED   hope

example: cherrie.RE.LA.VIR

should i listen to the VOICES in my HEAD

please don't   hurt me
                   hurt me
              hurt me
you're the only one   you're the only one
that lets me
                     i want to
hurt you   hurt me

☞ Just touch the screen and SCREAM✌RiV.etHEAD!
    Then: JUSTGOTOSLEEPJUSTO!TOSLEEP!w/

    • RE.LA.VIR Sleep Tips—PARK option

                 (i hope
                 you will
not pee on me.)

Immobilize RV.SEX, the RiV.etSEX.tinc hyperRE.ad environment,
by using the PARK option of the RE.LA.VIR MAIN MENU box.

RE.LA.VIR MAIN MENU

Edit
Park
Insert
He
Go to . . .
Toolbox
Windows
To return to . .
Shave . . .
She
Help balloons

☐ He
☐ Saves . . .

PARK provides five each of two types of VIR.tualVisUals (VIR.VUs) and/or VIR.tualVidEOs (VIR.VEOs):

Type I: ACT.iveForgetting

Type II: PASS.iveForgetting.

Specify:
- mode option: ACT.F or PASS.F
- type option: VIR.VUs or VIR.VEOs
- SPEED option:

constant: 0 to +10
variable: -∞ to +∞
fractal: $S(t) = S(t-1)^{**}(1/\text{ß})]$

ACTiveForgetting Options:

☐ CUT:[NOVEL: to]

☐ MORPHINEGLUE&YOU

☐ EATEATEATATDENNYS

☐ BODYTOOL&DIEME

☐ WD-40DYKES

PASSiveForgetting Options:

☐ I (Heart) MINIGOLF

☐ ABOATTOBALI

☐ THE19THCENT&ME

☐ JUSTGOTOSLEEPJUSTO!TOSLEEP

☐ JESUSLOVESMETHISIKNOW

☐ EVERYBODYSMILENOW

- Annotations

See:

> VIR.DIC.DOC.APPEND;D
> GLOSS.APPEND;A
> SOURCE.APPEND;B
> NARR.LIC&EXPLIC.APPEND;C

- System Enablers

See:

CODE.pendentmicrOProCESSORS	(CODE.OP.CESSORS)
LES.biannoMADS	(LES.MADS)
CHAR.acterCODEX	(CHAR.CODEX)
JIF.fyLUbe	(JIF.LU)
FoLLOW.T.hemfollowThem	(FLLOW.T.T)
MechA.nicPHyla	(MA.PH)
IT.inerantMEtallurgy	(IT.ME)
ID.entityS.amplingProgram	(ID.S.P)

- Display Control Panel Tips:

FIXLOCAT:	CUNT	LIMPET
	LEAF	
	LIPS	
	LOSS	

> DIAL 911   When no one comes then you know another now, a HYPER.RE.alNOW, rather than a VIR. tualNO.NO. NOVEL.NOW *he burns on the inside of your upper thigh with a cigarette.*

THIS CANNOT BE STOPPED BY PRESSING THE WHITE BUTTON.

He is still here.

CIRCUITS

He is still here.

SHIFTERS

He is still here.

wandering the G.R.I.D.

He is still here.
You let him in.
You let him in.

- SIMulations:

NOVEL%IN%IF%IT%DID%DID%%
IT   *didn't*
it   you   you   let   him in
NOVEL%IN%JUST%TO%DO%IT%
JUST%TO%DO%IT
you   did
      it
IN%IT%
didn't   you
IN
NOVEL%IN%SUPPOSE%IT%DID%
IT%IN
you
       et   him   in
NOVEL%IN%BE%NICE&QUIET%
IN
NOVEL%IN%HEATED%
IT%
NOVEL%IN%SPREAD
%OUT%LOUD
NOVEL%IN%DIS%OBE
DIANCE%TRAINING
NOVEL%IN
%STRAP%IT%ON&NOW
NOVEL%IN%SERVO
MOTOR%IN%NOVEL%IN%SO%GO%NOVEL%IN&FAST%FASTER%FAS
TEN%IN%SO%NOVEL%STRAP%IT%IN&KNEW&WHAT&IS%NEW%AB
OUT%NO%NO%NOVEL&IN%WHAT%TO%DO%WITH%IN%IT%NOVEL
%IN%IN%NNNN%TRODUC&F%IN%RED%F%IN%RED%F%IN%RED&I
N%NOVEL%WAYS%TO%NOVEL&IN&WEAR%IT%%IN%FER%TIL%LY
%IN%FUR%TIVE%LY%IN%NOVEL%USE%FUL%LY%IN%NOVEL%WAY
S%IN&THEN%TWO&THEN%OR%MORE%IN%ALL%WAYS&IN%IN%TH
IS%TOO&DO%THERE%IS%A%NOVEL%IN%THIS%TO&DO%THIS%TO
&IN%IN%TO&DIE%IN%TOOL%DIE%IN%TOOL&DIE%SISTERS%IN&N
OVEL&IN&WAYS%TOO%GIVEN%GIVEN%TOO%THE%F%NUMBER&N
O%VEL%ME%TOO%NO%NO%NO\\VEL&YES%I%WANT%IT%HERE%HA
VE%LA%LA%LARGER%B\ORE%IN%NO%NO%YES%NO%NOVEL%IN&T
WELVE%INCHES%IN%NOVEL\%IN%TRA%MUSC%U%LAR%OH%SO%W
ELL%OILED%JUNK&IE%NOVEL%IN%TOP&BOTTOM%TOO%STOP%S
TOP%IT%NOVEL%IN%IT%HURTS%STOP%IN%STOP%IT%ININ%&IN
%NOVEL%IN%STOP%IT%MALE&OR%FEMALE%OR%ININ%%NOVEL%
IN%NOVEL%IN% NOVEL%IN%STOP%IT%FUCK%IN%IN%NOVEL%INN

OVEL%TY%IN%FUCK%IN&IN%INAN%AN%GEL%NOVEL%FUCK%IN&
UP%UP%NOVEL%IN&UP%UP%UP%A%NOVEL%TY%IN&UP%HERASS
%%NOVEL%IN%A%NOVELTY%UP%HER%ASS%IN%ASK%HER%IN%IN
%A%NOVEL%IN%NAME%THIS%NAME%THIS%NOVEL%RE.LA.VIR%
WHAT%IS%THAT%THAT%IN%HER%THERE%THERE%RAM%THERE%
RAM%RAM%JUNKIE%IN%RAM%JUNKIE%IN%NOVEL%THERE%THER
E%MUST%BE%A%MILLION%NAMES%IN%IN%IN%IN%FOR%A%NO%
NO%NOVEL%IN%I%NARRATE%IN%NARRATE%OR%IN%EVERY%KIN
D%OF%NARRAPE%RAPE%RAPE&RATE%NARRAPE%RE.LA.VIR&RED
%RE.LA.VIR&RE.READ%ANOTHER%RAPE%IN%NOVEL%RAPE%IN%N
OVEL%NARRAPE%OR%OR%ORGAN%ORGAN%IZE%YOUR%NO%NO%
NOVEL%IN%ORGAN%EYES%YOUR%RAPE%IN%NOVEL%NARRATE%O
R%IS%THERE%ANY%DIFFERENCE%BETWEEN%NARRAPE%NARRATE
%DO%YOU%KNOW%ANY%NOVEL%TY%NO%KNOW%NOW%AND%N
OVEL%TO%THAT%IS%NOT%RAPE%I%KNEW%IT%WAS%NOT%NEW
%YOU%AND%ANY%BODY%PASSAGE%TO%NARRATE%IN%IN%NARR
APE%A%NOVEL%IN%RE.LA.VIR?

● ∞ NODES

1.	I DO NOT KNOW THE NOVEL I AM
2.	I DO NOT KNOW THE NOVEL I AM
3.	I DO NOT KNOW THE NOVEL I AM
4.	I DO NOT KNOW THE NOVEL I AM
5.	UNTIL
6.	I DO NOT KNOW THE NOVEL I AM
7.	UNTIL
8.	I DO NOT KNOW THE NOVEL I AM
9.	UNTIL
10.	I DO NOT KNOW THE NOVEL I AM
11.	UNTIL
12.	I AM RAPED

● ⊃————SUTURE Function

SUTURE is a mapping function which stitches a point from the
SmoothSpace(SS) of RE.LA.VIR to the body grid of the
BodY.CoORDinate (BY.CORD).

Examples:

```
I I I I I I I I I I
I HAVE A GUN I
I HAVE A GUN I
I HAVE A GUN I
```

```
I I I I I I I I I
I HAVE I HAVE I
I HAVE I HAVE I
I HAVE I HAVE I
I HAVE A FUCKING GUN
I HAVE A FUCKING GUN CUNT
ME AND MY FUCKING I GUN CUNT
I HAVE A I HAVE A FUCKING GUN CUNT
SO SPREAD AND CUNT GUN
SO FUCKING LICK MY GUN CUNT
SO SUCK IT CUNT I I I I I I
I HAVE A BIG FUCKING BIG FUCKING GUN CUNT
I HAVE A BIG FUCKING CUNT GUN
I HAVE A BIG GUN CUNT
I HAVE A BIG CUNT GUN
I AM BIG AND I HAVE A BIG FUCKING  GUN CUNT
I HAVE A GUN CUNT
I HAVE A GUN CUNT
I HAVE A GUNCUNT
I I I I I I I I I I I
```

If the System 7.1 Installation fails

RE.dLA.VIRtualhypernovel is made by machine because machines make no mistakes.

[NARRTRANS; <AUTOCONSMPTN>; RE.LA.VIRtualover is RE.ALly RE.ady made REadyMAde (A.RE.MA) RE.ALly RE.MAke.ME by machines because machines make no mistakes.]

Memory (RAM.MEMO.REX//ROM.ME.MA.REX):

Make no mistakes.
Make no mistakes.
Make no mistakes.

Examples:

Example 1:

I stroke her hair. She moves away. I make tea. I bring it to her on a pretty tray with our best tea cups and our kitty cat creamer. I bring her the Honey Bear and a plate of Milano cookies.

"You smell like sex," she says, while I pour

the tea.

                  I tape a photograph of two women entwined
to the sand.

             Example 2:

                  I HAVE A GUN
                  I HAVE A CUNTGUN
                  I HAVE A GUN
                  I HAVE A GUN
                  I HAVE A CUNTGUN
                  I HAVE A GUN
                  I HAVE A CUNTGUN
                  I HAVE A CUNTGUN

             Example 3:

                  DEAR queenie,

                  FUCKIN DEAD BITCH FUCKIN DEAD BITCH CUNT
                  FUCKIN FUCK TIL YOU DIE TIL YOU'RE DEAD
                  DEAD DEAD

                  LOVE,

                  WILL YOU REMEMBER ME IF WE MEET AGAIN
                  IN PARADISE

eof

PARK.RV: PASSF5/EVERYBODYSMILENOW
&LINK: APPEND//XXX.DOC:
WHOSAIDNEEDSADIC.DOIGOTADICIGOTADICDOCIGOTAIGOTADIC
DOCIGOTADICDICIGOTADIC
IGOTADICIGOTADICDOCIGOTAIGOTADICDOCIGOTADICDICIGOTA
DIC:

⊗⊗⊗

              RE.LA.VIR   oβoλUTILItyBox
⊗⊗0

   ☞ FEM.aleejacULATOR(FEM.ULATOR)

           This 22" model has outstanding connectivity. Old
           serial ports just can't keep up. This 300x300 dpi
           monster is built tough to take the pounding. Applicat-

ion diversity you've come to expect from RiV.et SEX.tinc. Includes: lakes, rivers, streams, waterfalls, dams, canals, shore-lines, railways, depots, railyards, and more! Comes with FM synthesizer and EtherNet Wave Technology. Includes a free CD. Easy installation—you'll be up and running in just a few minutes!

P22-1001	Ovation 820
	(single user)
P22-1002	Ovation 840
	(two users)
P22-1010	Ovation 900
	(up to ten users)

☞ LatexDataGlove(LDG)

Worried about viruses? Just use a disposable LDG. All you need for safe digital text(s)! XS, S, M, L, XL, XXL. Also available in gift-edition leather. Specify black or white. Digital extenders available: 8-bit or 16-bit. Comes in dispenser boxes of 100 LDGs.

☞ NARR.ativeoRgAn.ProbE (NARR.RAPE)

Scan your brains out with RV.SEX expand/collapse, Show&Tell internal O! mnIN.ME scanner. With Reli2400DPI subject/object orientations, NARR.RAPE has you up and MasterNarrative sizzling with resolution in no time! Features Yank&Place manipulation of body parts, sound bites, B&W and full-color image clips, and text brush effects like blur, sharpen, and grayscale. Just give it an image and hold on—it can be pretty exciting! NARR.RAPE comes in two models—the Internal 8Xi and the Portable 8Xp. Each kit includes cables, jacks, scan wand, and sample pack of NOMOS™(RiV.etSEX.tinc):machine-oiled probesleeves. 8Xp kit includes dual rechargable powerpacks. NARR. RAPE requires modem port. Please specify: textured or smooth, all natural vegetable material or heavy metal, double- or single-headed, beaded or un-, hand held or strap-on, size (fixed lenth models: 10", 12", 15"; or variable-length telescope model), and color. NO ANIMAL TESTING USED!

VO7-1002	Internal 8Xi.
	100% safe for use with mechanical devices. Also available: the MultiSpin 8Xi.
VO7-1003	Portable 8Xp.

Use the 8Xp at home, in the office, or on the go. This little speedster pours on the power—with blistering fast 450 KB per second. You gotta see it to believe it!

VO7- 1120   NARR.RA.PE Accessories Kit:
HERE IS WHAT YOU GET:
How to CUM.PLOT—CD-ROM
STOP&GEL—CD-ROM
Power Surge Console
Paradise Accelerator 2.4

☞ LA.VIR.tualnovelHYPErCHAir(LA.VIR.HYPECHA)
Full-body strap-in environment selects, organizes, invents and engineers movement, sound, electronic disturbance, and the active discharge of each WRI.Der's novel postorganic physical zones of penetration and interpenetration. Smooth spaces (ss), and multipositional G.R.I.D.s(GRrrrr) of relative domination and subjugation in the privacy of the individual WRI.Der's own subjectivity. Compliant with RE.LA.VIR,LDG, FEM.ULATOR, NARR.RA.PE, LA.VIR.HYP CHA, FiberScope (FS), and TRANS.GLOBE. (U.P.S. only. Allow 3 weeks for delivery.)

☞ FiberScope
For examination of inaccesible areas, as in:

I DO NOT KNOW THE WOMAN I AM
I DO NOT KNOW THE WOMAN I AM
I DO NOT KNOW THE WOMAN I AM
I DO NOT KNOW THE WOMAN I AM
UNTIL
I DO NOT KNOW THE WOMAN I AM
UNTIL
I DO NOT KNOW THE WOMAN I AM
UNTIL I DO NOT KNOW THE WOMAN
I AM UNTIL I DO NOT KNOW
I AM
I DO NOT KNOW
I AM
THE WOMAN
THE WOMAN
THE WOMAN
I AM
I AM
I AM UNTIL
I DO NOT KNOW

I DO NOT KNOW UNTIL
I AM
THE WOMAN I AM UNTIL I DO NOT KNOW
I DO NOT KNOW I
I DO NOT KNOW I
AM
AM I
I AM THE WOMAN
I AM
I DO NOT KNOW THE WOMAN I AM
UNTIL

☞ TRANS.parentGLOBE (TRANS.GLOBE)
    Until clearly she is seen to be UNTIL I AM
SEEN TO BE an apparatus I SEE MYSELF AS AN APPARATUS to
be fed TO BE FED to be force fed TO BE FORCED AND FED to be
forced and fed spherical TO BE FORCED and TO BE FORCED
and TO BE FORCE FED and FORCED FED SPHERICAL to be so
narrated and so raped SO NARRATED I AM SO NARRATED I AM
SO NARRAPED so named AND NAMED a Woman NAMED SO
WOMAN NAMED SO WOMAN I AM NOT NAMED WOMAN CUNT
in a glass sphere LOOK AT ME I AM NOT CUNT IN A GLASS
SPHERE IN

   AS NARRATED

        OR

That's it. Enjoy RE.LA.VIR!

eof

cut:[novel:to

NO.NO:[NOVEL: CUNT TO::

SIM2\RE.LA.VIR:

HOWRED

HOW TO SUR
VIVE: RE.LA.
VIR

----

a novel WRI.De
by

Howred A. Acton

```
_____cumplot_
__|___|_____
__|___|_____|___|_____
                            __|___|_____
suture            __|___|_____

____cumplot_____cumplot_____
_____cumplot
```

cumplot

Welcome to TEMPL.NARR.RAPE!

You have just entered TEMP.NARR.RAPE.

To establish your location in HOWRED.RE.LA.VIR's
TEMPL.NARR.RAPE just touch the screen.

FIXLOCAT: CUNT

OPENing...

SCREE.REAL: VIR.VEO: FUCKED TIL SHE

☐ FUCKED TIL SHE

☐ FUCKED TIL SHE

He turns on the screen

☐ FUCKED TIL SHE

he proceeds to torture you with his narration:

☐ FUCKED TIL SHE

he severs the sinews near your heels, and then opens your
belly from which he draws the heart, liver, spleen and
lungs, which he sticks on an iron hook, and cuts and dis-
sects into pieces, which he then sticks on other hooks as he
cuts them, as one does with an animal.

you are a part now

DIAL 911

no one comes

THIS CANNOT BE STOPPED BY PRESSING THE WHITE BUTTON

☞ just touch the screen

HA; HA. There's no conflict between us now.

a whole NETwork of TV viewers

watch
you

a body effaced

I watch you

her eyes   as you deface my body   your eyes

as you deface my body

you say:

you say: watch me   you say: I am   the next

woman.   I am this

woman   trembling   animal.

I am   this I woman   I am   discussing

disgusting

disgusting   me.

me.

he cranks and cranks and clicks you wider and wider.

you say: "Who are you?"   "I am the woman who

was raped."   you say:

I do not know.   I do not know   the woman   I am. I do

not know   the woman until   I am raped.   I do not

know the woman   I am until I am   raped. I am   not dead

but I am

separated.

PARK.ME//PASSF.ME:THE19THCENTURY&ME

The woman arrives by train with a suitcase. She is here to replace you.

You make arrangements to meet her at the station. You leave your child with a friend. She has a child the same age as your son.

It is snowing outside.

She says, "I heard there could be snow tonight. Be care-

ful."

Outside it is snowing.

In her kitchen outside the window snow has buried everything, the streets are snow dunes.

The man sitting at the table is reading a foreign language newspaper, the paper is so thin the light from the lamp on the table shines through. It is French.

He is not unattractive. He occupies his own narrow zone geometrically defined by the two planes of the newspaper intersecting with the two planes of the kitchen wall and the table top.

There are six doors. All of them are bolted.
It is snowing outside.

You try to think of some perfectly innocent remark you once made you could make once more again some remark spoken as if she were of no importance as if you were now owned jointly by two women rather than one put up for public display, used by shop windows, by passengers passing entering and leaving her the station, you,

I said, "The trip has made me hungry." I say, "The trip has made me hungry." You say, "The trip has made me hungry."

But she is afraid to speak. She is afraid to speak she is afraid to say this you say this. I am. I am. I am.

I am the woman who was raped.

The man does not reply. He makes some indescribably familiar gesture. Neither of you move. You together form between you one two three an exact imitation of the man and the woman and the other any other woman. The man's upper body is framed by the woman's and the other woman has slipped in between this is impossible the man receding, a woman flailing, perpendicular, this woman is your reflection in the window. The windows are equidistant. The distance between them is identical.

The man's head is turned toward the window. You cannot see what he sees outside of the window. I will tell you on the other side of the window is a series of equidistant windows. He sees a series of equidistant windows. The distance between each of them is identical. Inside there are no blinds he can see inside each blindless window he can see through the metal grates bolted to each window he can see bolted to each window a metal grate bolted to each floor a metal bed. There are no women in the windows yet. There are no women on the beds yet.

am.i disappearing btwn columns

Parallel to this there is a woman outside standing outside in the snow. She is standing outside on the snow-covered sidewalk where the snow-covered driveway meets the wrought iron gate. The wrought iron gate is closed, bolted. There are three inches of snow on each horizontal surface of the wrought iron fence. The fence is twelve-and-one-half feet high. The stone walls of a nineteenth century station are visible through the wrought iron gate. The train has not arrived yet. There are no women on the beds yet. The policeman at the desk shifts a piece of paper from the right side of the desk to the left side of the desk. A telephone is ringing and ringing and ringing.

I wake from the dream of another person. Now I can wash her face, eat her breakfast, and feel secure that I was not raped even though I can still smell the man's rancid hair as I struggle to perceive my real body while symbols float around me: windows, trains, snowplows, the cat walking on the table.

I do not know. I do not know the woman I am. I do not know until I am raped. I do not know the woman I am until I am raped. I am not dead but I am separated.

I work this ambiguous miracle: I wake from the dream of another person.

The woman is arriving by train. She is here to replace you. Ten women are arriving by train. They are here to replace you. They arrive one by one at the wrought iron gate. They are deposited at the station by some intermittant engine that like the snowplow experiences engine difficulty. It starts. It stops. It starts. It stops. It is an erratic progression through an unfamiliar landscape which appears sometimes lunar in its desolation, sometimes cracked pavement abandoned long enough ago that weeds have had time to grow foot high between the cracks, sometimes wind-born dust or snow blows up in funnel-shaped clouds obscuring the traveler's view of her passage so that it is hard to say if it is one long passage or one long steady climate in a jar. The storms are of indeterminate length, even the progress of the sun is obscured so that night is indistinguishable from day, and the traveler who has been etching her face on the window for some sign of human habitation, a station, a house, a fence post, a cat, sees in the window only her own lines in a piece of glass, visible writing suggesting nothing, thinks it is during these times that what she is here to replace exists at some station, but she missed it.

The man looking out the window sees across the courtyard a harshly illuminated zone, there is a statue of a marble woman recumbent prone not at ease in this position on her back struggling to rise against a violent force perhaps a strong wind or a fast river or an express train. Her arms are raised, palms up, fingers spread wide. The snow accumulates in her palms. She is frozen in a pose of rising, not risen, resisting, the snow is falling. The snow collects in the palms of her hands, in the folds of her belly and thighs.

The man says, "Of course you cannot sleep here."

The wallpaper itself is not something that must be repeated. It is simply a pattern of repeating feathers which are either floating up or floating down, the direction is impossible to determine.

Outside, there is the sound of the snowplow. It is experiencing engine trouble. A scraping sound, a sputter, a ceasing of scraping, a ceasing of sputtering, then the series repeats itself. It is a sequence of cause, effect, cause cause effect effect effect, cause effect cause effect cause cause then a long pause effect pause effect, it sputters like this slowly down the street to the intersection.
The driver curses.
The woman standing at the gate observes in the blinking yellow lights the ineffectual progress of the snowplow which is experiencing engine difficulty, the steady accumulation of snow on the suitcase she is holding.

She is too little, too late.

But still, I have this ugly little story to report:
A black sedan approaches the intersection. The light is red. The five men in the black sedan see a woman standing alone in front of the station. It is snowing. The red light turns green. She hears the tires spin in the snow. The driver curses.

It's much later now.
It's done.
The flashing light of the snowplow lit orange the snow that edged the wrought iron railing, the branches of the trees that separately seemed distant, together, they, as a group, closed around her.

In the kitchen, the man turns a page.

Let me tell you about nightmares:
for a while I identify myself with this being: The Woman

Who Was Raped. For a while I identify with what they do to her body.

Let me tell you about nightmares:
Here is the end. Her spine without order. Her sentence breaks on the horizon. She makes notes on the roof, the pipes have burst. How things are passing through her throat: ships, globes, seas, jungles. Your hand keeps pressing against her glass ribcage. What has happened to the story of her body, intimate as shop windows. One has every chair burning, they roll, they gallop. One's friends always come to call. The place was empty. One asks, "How does she behave with gloves on her hands?" The girl sits from dawn to dusk, from dusk to dawn to dawn.

Here is the end.
Now let us sing dancing up and down on the horizon.
The structure is now. Do not move. Do not go. She points with her gloved hand at her breast bared. There are figures without features, two figures wrapped in gas-fire, so fluid has my body become. Change is possible. I choose the armchair and a few gasometers. I hate ceremonies.

After our fire we are extinct.

I like to sleep now.

She has replaced me.

This is a real Madwoman talking to you now.
"I've had enough of this lunar movement that makes me name what I refuse and refuse what I have named."

I am the Madwoman from Paradise.

For a while I identify myself with this being: The Woman Who Was Raped. Then, I work this ambiguous miracle: I cease to identify with what they do to my body. The woman who was raped. Has ceased to exist.

I like to sleep now.

She is gone.

Now I can escape the eye that is watching me, he is always watching me, do you know what I mean, I think you do know what I mean by his face is always at the window. Let me

tell you about nightmares.
But first I'd like to talk about Paradise. Paradise. This is a real Madwoman talking to you: one who knows happiness in the world now that she has left it.

Paradise: there, I work this ambiguous miracle: I refuse to identify with what they do to her body. Weary of being wrongly and uselessly blown up and out of shape, my body pulls itself together in a kind of immeasurable hunger.

"The trip has made me hungry, hungry, hungry."

He tries to touch me with his agile, sinewy hands.

☞ok   just

YOU TRY

If this is what you want this is what you get if this is what you want this is what you get if this is what you want this is what you get this is what you get this is what you get this is what want you want get what you want want if this is what you want [Repeat 7X]

you see what I mean?

(rape,
she said),

(narrative,
he said)

microME.NU.TEMPL.NARR.RAPE&EXECUTE ▼ touch the SCREEn

☐ Dec. 1988: EXECUTE

        needle popped out of arm

        of _____ & sprayed all

        over the room;   we pulled the curtain.

he la

47 min. to locate a vein <u>Billy Wayne Right.</u>

<u>Steven Ray</u> inside the orange

bars of the

execution cell

❑ try: his lips turn blue

then he stops moving

❑ that was too easy

for <u>Steven</u> to just be put to sleep

PARK:PASSF:JUSTGOTOSLEEPJUSTO!TOSLEEPJUSTGOTOS
LEEPJUSTO!TOSLEEPJUSTGOTOSLEEPJUSTO!TO
SLEEP!the world that surrounds you is only an idea only a
SIMulacrum forced onto a wider and wider and wider SCREE.REAL

Φ IVAN you bad bad   bad terrible boy

                              boy

we're taut now and disciplined

then why did you choose her

Little Red Eye: Little Red Eyelet I let leave
Little Red Eye: Leather & Latex, hear her, bend over form
and semblance you you

a double presence of climax and mirror
          Little Red Eye Eye
                    Eye Eye

he watches you

Little REd neon Eye-Eye

CAM&CORDher

SHOW RE.ALTI.ME: VIR.VEO

❏ I'M NOT THE SAME

FIXLOCAT: ☞ LIM.PET

VIR.DIC.DOC: Find: <u>LIM</u>pet

very young very disturbing
in the littoral areas
clings very tightly when disturbed

LIGHTS CAMERA ACTION by HOW.RED ACT.ON

VIR.VEO:ME.NU:

❏Imagine a Little RE.d LEAF upon a scene

❏ any where

❏ there

❏ is an ocean still &

❏ a wish for

6:03 am i.am tied&tightly in the littoral areas

❏ Imagine a

©©
Stop Depth Dive Time Dive Time Depth and Mode: Surf Hist
©©
By the distant light of flares
I could see the young woman standing there in an unlined
dress with long sleeves, hiding her face with a fan as she sang,

Little RE.d LEAF Little RE.d LEAF Little   Little RE.d LEAF

It was a very moving sight.

I called for her boat to be rowed alongside ours.

She was accompanied by a boy dressed in a scarlet underrobe of glossy silk, a hunting cloak of light purple with green lining, and figured red silk trousers.

I called for him to be bound to the railing and masked while I parted her on the deck, and embuggered her. I then ordered the boy's red silk trousers be lowered and I proceeded to embugger him.

I have never seen a parting equal to the beauty of this scene— the pine branches, the sky all shrouded by mist, the surface of the sea, the waves breaking on the beach.

I composed this dissertation I ordered taken down:

> Men's preferences when they resort to libertinage, we might, in order mostlucidly to examine the question reduce those tastes to three: sodomy, sacriligious fancies, and penchants to cruelty. The first of these passions is universal today; to what we have already said upon it we shall join a few choice reflections. It divides into two classes: ACTive and PASSive: the man who embuggers, be it boy, be it woman, acquits himself of an active sodomization; he is a PASSive SODOMitE when he has himself buggered.

duh duh duhduh   duh
duh diddid duhdidduh didduhdid uh did
     marquisduhsahdsaythat   yeah so

PASS.SO.DO.DO.DO.MEN.U:

❏ O I(heart)VANtheMANifoldTEMPLateDYKE!

   ❏TEMPL.TOOL&DIE&TOOL&DIE&TO OL&TOOL&DIE.ME
                                             <she does me new>

she loosens my legs, lifts me up by the scarf and tugs in slow jerks as i pivot to my knees. i can't sit down so i go from an
          upright kneel on the bed with a little
      jump both feet are on the floor and despite the
      move i must make she holds firm and two knots
      slip out, a large and a small

Welcome to TEMPL: Stop it.
FUCKINGBITCHCUNTWHOBUTTFUCKSTHEDEAD!   You're
dead

                                                    bitch
                                        Loosen up.
        NO.NO.NOvel went NOva.   I try but I can't.

        The small one goes in easy.   She strokes my anus
with more lube.   my lower rectum is full of black
                    silk
and the big one she   until I relax with rolls around and
around   then presses the metal head in to   Good girl
Get up and get   I have decided to specialize in_____.

me a joint. The scarf   my rectum fast before i know it
                    i know it   has happened it is in. She
hanging entrail she   How authoritarian structures run
                              keeps the tension on it
holds as i   wild in this utopian moment   follows me

                                        Let's go to the
bathroom.

                    She sets up the _____.
i let her push it in   camcorder

        There are no spatio-temporal constellations to
twelve oiled knots into   over
        map. There are no spatio-temporal constellations at
my anus. The insertion   the toilet
    all. Only random holes in this inverted black of the
13th and largest knot   Bend down
    bowl. Sometimes the holes fall down. Sometimes I lose
control

it's painful and i cry   in front of
        I tear the sides of your mouth   the fucking tub
                              Spread&Splay Bitch
        when I ejaculate you cry out loud there's this rip
            and out slides a very REd planet   Are you ready
now Bitch
She ties a long silk scarf

            Here suck on this   No.
very slowly while I watch her   Don't watch.
        maybe it's the birth of   Eat.
anus with more lube.   I don't want him to watch

eat

DON'T WATCH!

EAT

My lower rectum is full of black   GO AWAY !
silk.   Get up and GET THE BIG BLACK ONE BITCH!
 She unties my leg, lifts
me up by the silk a knot slips out   WALK!   another
 bigger knot slides out   IS THAT WHAT YOU WANT   I say
                    IS THAT WHAT YOU WANT

HOW.RED
 yes that is what I want.   a BIG BLACK DICK UP MY ASS & a
silk scarf too   I help her

4STIMulation/She Watches Channel Φ

☞ just touch the screen

                    I think I needed it.
                    Suppose I did I needed it.

REAL.TI.ME: 2:03 am.i

     ❑ NO.NO.NOvel in if it did.
It did.
          ❑NO.NO.NOvel in just to write butt
fuckedbuttfuckbuttfuckedb
     uttfucked&buggered   butt butt button em
          buggered butt butt   buttffff sss butff ss fss
snakeroot butt buttfuck   192
                    protrude   a pug protrusion
                              a pussy
                                vulva usu.
                                   considered vul
                              gar
                                BUTTFUCK
                              pussyfoot
                              pussytoes

                         buttFUCK
                    a WHOREy composition
     ❑ NO.NO.NOvel in object one rigid texts.
                              be my be in
                              my BAND i'm

calling "PUSSY
TOES?"
let's call that
panther what's
her name ___.
hope
right beside a
stuffing box
containing oil

What kind of
STiMUTILATio
n is THAT

turboRAMJET
you won't get
any dates like
THAT way girl.

grrrrrl, can't get enough of that old rugged

❏ NO.NO.NOt that

❏ NO.NO.NOvel in medium-sized fistfuck fis
tfuckfistfuckfis
tfuckedfistfucked&embuggered.

❏ NO.NO.NOvel in piss
pissss pissssspisssssssssssonmebitch
❏ NO.NO.NOvel in lift your fat leg &

fart ❏ NONONO velinspreadyourfatass ❏ NONONO.VEL in

whendidyoueatlast   a wholebabyasswhole❏ NO.NO.
NO.VEL in supposididsupposididanenemalittleglycerine

❏NO.NO.NOvel in so ffffffffsssssfsssfssssssss
fsssfsstfstfssssttssssfstfc k me in the ass please now, I am
cleansed,
          Madame.

❏ NO.NO.NOvel in so GO. GO.

❏NO.NO.NOvel in stop

❏ Stop!

SO WHYTHEFUCKD'YOUSTOP BITCH

Since I could hardly leave her alive, deflowered
Little Red Leaf, I order the boy to disembowel her with his
sword. He does as I order. We leave her body on the beach
below the golden gaze of

❑ TEMPL.PINKGLYPH&CLIFF

she was only nineteen, very young, very disturbing

I keep gazing back as we row away thinking I could never
get enough of

 you

AUDIO:FOGHORN

        I work this ambiguous miracle: I choose the room that
corresponds to my desires rather than that which corresponds
to my fears.

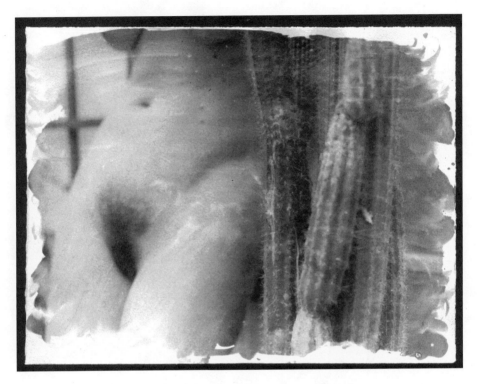

I work this ambiguous miracle

Imagine the time before the time before the red leaf fell, summer an a priori green and sunny swath summer yes yes yes and yes yes and no no reason not to furrow day by day day day after day a willing green not to change this lake season really summer every summer summer summer summer summer summer summer summer they had come to this lock lake season and loss.

If they have not boarded a steamer.

One of the girls, she is a lovely, passionate thing tilting her head upward thoughtfully as she chews a blade of grass, says, "Why is history?"

This has started as in winter.

"What's happening to us?"

The sound of apples.

There is the occasional sound of a ship's horn.

"You'll move to LA and you'll change."

Ermine could be a color.

"What about me?"

Alice you you too could be a color.

"You'll forget about me."

How do you say Forgotten forget.

"Red, remember?"

Remember interruptedly might just be more connected color to concentrate on what could happen in the pale name alone novel, RE.d, a virtual making love to continue you and her coming in between pattern this watercolor patter between our thighs and your tongue slips into elaborate sables which open alternative arrangements the pink tuberose in between what a half a cliff to connectedly.

Connected to you can always be red and river boats and not a hypernovel RE.LA.VIR to see and to see and to see in between air palms to be connected to any even beautiful grey thud and fog. RE.d. See. Always see these beginning frames, transcortical paths to, video clouds and TEMPLes that populate and fly us.

I jet from sea to sea to see her every cup I long for is
RE.d RE.d redundancy and wait.

The telephone rings in virtually every novel read about
fluorescent women. We are not fluorescent women.

"The story—how did we run out of it."

In the parking lot, our wheels about to implode in love
in speculation things were different now the things that make
us us free free us in form how many names have we known
easily without a doubt in a moment of emergency people swarm
off the pavement

Wait! Wait! the woman says I need some help things go
from bad to worse there are two possibilities: either she gets
raped in the front seat of the black sedan or I devise another
architecture in which I do not foreshorten my own ending, this
a read novel virtual hyper red red NO NO NOvel not to die to.

SIM3\RE.LA.VIR:
cherrie

my new life

---

a NO.NO.NOvel by

cherrie s.

VIR.VUs: RED MULTIPLE WINGED THINGS
[INSERT]

Reader	I am not	an	optical	appliance
Reader	I am not	an	optical	appliance
Reader	I am not	an	optical	appliance
Reader	I am not	an	optical	appliance
Reader	I am not	an	optical	appliance

Reader, I am not an optical appliance.

Imagine the first splash of RE.d is a little opening to everything you can possibly imagine about despair, about violence, about anonymity, about hope, about hope, about color like a probable climax in vegetation fluorescent vegetation equidistant from origin and death, in the middle of a white screen, BLANK!

(read for more than REd)

the gliding season torn open space and saying something smooth and neon red against the sky says:

EAT   EAT   EAT

you blink and some day some body you think some day some body will it will it will it will it mean this: say "Some Day Some Body Might Spring."

. . . .

TEMPL:PETRO!GLYPHGRRRRRLs:microME.
NU

. . . .

⬚ Chapter, one pavement, matter, form, and Spring too

Welcome to _____ !

O.K. Little REd LEAF   here we are:
☞ just touch the screen
                                  cunt

❏ Chapter__ & two or three mammals . . .

1. a new age of life . . .

Imagine your human body is a little mammal word a little mammal world about to novel into gender race and class a little boat broke about to redden ark in to two or three every broken pieces of its spine this very large wreck and RE.d civilization is it possible is it possible to imagine human skin RE.ad on the horizonal sky a sentence to the fragmentation of it the skin the sky the color body and the sun rising quietly oppressed with no organs the sun quiet a body with no organs rising and leaving leaving with no organs and rising rising again & again still with no organs RE.d over RE.d RE.d smooth space (ss).

Smooth and smooth space (sss ss) the sea the secret (shhhh) body already born to the body sea see it's alRE.ady born and after birth. This little RE.d LEAF, not a genesis, it's afloat and float, it's a little RE.d desert bloom, at middle of its life, it's adrift of sand and sand, and see it's STILL all RE.ady a little RE.d LEAF upon a scene and boatless it's a little RE.d boatless with no organs—every stable bit of it—thud and fog, branch and leaf, at first it was all organic and then it was all window glass, window willow, window pine, spine, glass and then it is all metallic, glitterati and shrapnel—you have to tell about what gets lost, what gets taken from your mouth, what was never in there, and the flavor of your blood, this RE.d wet noun neon RE.d piercing your tongue.

It is a navigational nightmare.

See! what this nine-inch nail carves on the inside of your SCREEn.

....

2. tradition comes into the world.

....

I DO NOT KNOW THE NOVEL I AM UNTIL ❏

I DO NOT KNOW THE NOVEL I AM UNTIL ❏

you're

I DO NOT KNOW THE NOVEL I AM UNTIL ❏   STUPID!

I DO NOT KNOW THE NOVEL I AM UNTIL ❏

you're
STUPID!

***THIS NOVEL SUCKS__O.K. MR A B C MAN MR IF A and B then C MAN—HERE I AM TO ORGAN.ON YOU All HELLO WESTERN CIVILIZATION BEGINS HERE HERE WITH ME HERE HERE I AM I AM MR ArisTOTLE Man, MR AM I AM THEREFORE I AM MR CAT-EGORY MAN I WILL CATEGORY YOU I WILL NOUN AND VERB AND PREDICATE YOU JUST WATCH ME SYLLO-GISM YOU (HELP HELP ME SCATTERGORIES!) MR LADY WHO ARE YOU MAN A WOMAN IF YOU'RE NOT A STRAIGHT WHITE MAN THEN BEND THE FUCK OVER AND I'LL EDUCATE YOU YOU CAN'T THINK RIGHT THINK RIGHT YOU CAN'T ALIKE ME MAN AND I'll MAKE YOU THINK RIGHT RIGHT AND TRUE I GOT THE RIGHT AND TRUTH TOO GET IT STRAIGHT MAN BEGIN AT THE BEGINNING WHAT'S THE BEGINNING THE BEGINNING IS WHAT COMES OH I KNOW ALL ABOUT THAT SHUT UP NO YOU DON'T KNOW ANY-THING ABOUT ANYTHING SHUT UP DON'T MOVE I'M GONNA EDUCATE ALIKE SO HERE SUCK THIS: THE BEGINNING IS WHAT COMES AFTER WHAT HAS COME BEFORE IS COMPLETELY OVER THE PRIOR COMPLETED THING THAT CAME BEFORE IS AND SO THAT'S THE ENDING THE ENDING IS THE COMPLETED THING THE WHOLE COMPLETED THING THAT MAKES IT AN ENDING AND THE MIDDLE IS WHAT COMES IN BETWEEN THE BEGINNING AND THE ENDING IT COMES BEFORE THE ENDING AFTER THE BEGINNING SUCK IT BITCH

CAN I BEGIN MY NOVEL NOW

❏I DO NOT KNOW THE NOVEL I AM UNTIL

❏ I DO NOT KNOW THE NOVEL I AM UNTIL

❏I DO NOT KNOW THE NOVEL I AM UNTIL

❏ I DO NOT KNOW THE NOVEL I AM UNTIL

Chapter: VOIRs talking in the G.R.R.R.R.I.D. . . . (should i
                                            listen to
                                            the voices
                                            in my head?)

"After all, who can challenge replicated causality?"

"I have my doubts even about corporeal things."

"queenie, I loved the little house on the archipelago, the aqua door, la porte a paradise."

"It's hard to remember, then, you know, another now."

"queenie, if, only for a day, if only for a day, if, only, for, a, day, i had her if only for a day I had enough queenies for a day now, now if you had now enough queenies for a large enough day now if you had enough large enough queenie a large enough one now if only for a large enough day day you had a large enough today and a boat too, a whole ferry of large enough for a day to, see, and you do, queenie, you probably do to, you probably do to, see, if, then, if then if if the identities of both are n then convergent in imagine a little red leaf upon a scene and i do imagine a little red leaf upon a scene anywhere there is an ocean still and a wish for a stable season, and, queenie, i so wish for a stable season, the REALity a set of SEEMIngly related equations to imagine to a little REd LEAF upon an equation w/ independent variables:"

VIRtual boat(1); VIRtual boat(2):

some nouns	some verbs
arrangements	xxxxx
weeding	xxx
"a noun means	he said sense"
farewell	measure

I III III III I I Imathematical theories of identityI III III III I I

(i never really
planned to tell
you a story)

$$y = \approx\approx\approx\approx\approx\approx\approx \quad + \qquad\qquad + \qquad + \ldots$$

sine   wave
cosine   wave

bye bye

$$\ldots + I + I = I \qquad\qquad OR$$

$$\Psi = \sum_{N=0}^{\infty} I_N = I_1 + I_2 + \ldots + I_N + \varepsilon_N$$

where:
  I, I, and I =   1. ICON ICON ICON;
                   2. ΦI.VAN☞ you know the one
                                      the Terrible
                   3. I I CON; III IIII   II IIII   IIII III
                   4. SIM STIMUS STIM ISIT HIM STIM
                   5. 2 QUEENIES AND A BROKEN TO; and
                   6. THIS TOO THIS BODY FOR A DAY;
  and   7. I I I; and/or
                   8. I/DENT/I/FY; with
                   9. THIS RED, NOW, I IDENTIFY WITH;
                   10. THIS, RED, QUEENIE; and this
                   11. cunt, to,
                       .
                       .
                       .
                   N. NONONOvel CUNT: [NOVEL: to]
  and ε   =   ≈ ≈ ≈ ≈ ≈ ≈ ≈ ≈ ≈ ≈ ≈   .   .   .   ∞
      N

TEMPLmacroMENU: WOMENWARMACHINE!

Chapter: Runic Writing by the First Women Like Us

....

     3. The near and far, and the extreme or vacuum range
     4. Female human horns
     5. The first appearance of fur and feather . . .
----

4. Female human horns

I hear them—whoever they are—
                              BOWOOOOOOOoooooooo
something on the verge of—
                              BOWOOO-BOWOOOOO
as in dialogue, appetite, the clatter of wheels upon the tracks
who are they
                              BOWOO-wo-wo-wo-
what did they lose, what
                              WOOOO-WOOoooooo
did they look like.

TEMPL.atelASSes::VIRVID//WOMENWARMACHINE!1:   ΦI

III:

queenie
(the drug that cares more)

(her secret ___ is:)   <u>password</u>

(buttfuckme)

IV:

am.i.queenieII

O!I!Φ!IIDONOTKNOWTHISIDONOTKNOWTHISIDONOTWANTTHISID
ONOTWANTTHISIDONOTKNOWTHISIDONOTWANTTHISIDONOTDO
THISIDONOTWANTTHISDONOTDOTHISIDONOTDOTHISDONOTW
ANTTHISIDOTHISIDOTHISI

V:

am.i.queenie.raped

(her secret ___ is:)

ΦIIDO!NO!TKNO!WTHEWOMANIAMUNTILIDO!NO!TKNO!WTHEWO
MANIAMUNTILIDO!NO!TKNO!WTHEW.MANIAMUNTILIDO!NO!TKNO
!WUNTILI!AM!RAPED!

- TEMPL.RE.MNEUmonics

TEMPL.RE.MNEUmonics::TEMPL.RE.ME.NEUmonics::RE.NU
E.ME.monics::I   need   a   new   name
for____.::TEMPL.ME::RE.NUE.monicME ::GET ME OFF THIS
FUCKING SACRIFICIAL BLOCK::TELL&TELL::SH OW&TELL::I'M
NOT GOING TO FUCKING SHOW&TELL::WHAT THEY DID TO MY
BODY::I need a new name for____.::WE NEED A NEW NAME
FOR____WHAT   THEY   DID   TO   YOUR
BODY::RE.NUE.monicME::RE.ME::RE.RE.ME::RE.RE
.adME::RE.&RE.&   RE.ME::remember
me?::RE.RE.MEMBER.ME::RE.MEMBER HIM:: HE. PNEU.mo nic::MR.
S.P. A.M::MR.SPerm&Anti freezeMan::CAN YOU IDENTIFY
HIM::YOU:: YOU remember::ALL OF YOU::remember
Y O U & Y O U & Y O U & Y O U & Y O U
RAPED&RAPED&RAPED&RAPED&RAPE D raped and raped and
rape   dme::(I   don't   think   so)::MFWRM
::MOTHERFUCKINGWHITERAPEMACHINE:: (I don't think so)

TEMPL.RE.MNEUmonics are acronymn(s) (of up to 16 characters) that assist the memory in the recording, storing, recalling, and manipulating of continuously variable visual quantities.

> example 1: RE.LA.VIR

> RE.dLA.VIRtualred, read, imagine, a little red leaf (you read leaf) upon a scene anywhere there is an ocean still and a wish for a stable season.

> example 2: TEMPLRE.EFWORLD

> Let's just pick any boat—they all go to the same fucking place: RE.EFWORLD!

> RE.dLA.VIR.tualIF.WORLD and a boat about, any boat about, to, just pick any fucking boat about, they all go to the same fucking place.

> ❑ ABOATABOUT

> • VIR.tualVIsionARIES(VIR.VIARIES)

[NARR.TRANS.EXPLIC: In Bomba en route to Altun Ha on a river we disembark to board a van. There is a stand selling wood carvings made in the jungle river village. I buy two carved zircote shells, one finished, one unfinished. There is only one unfinished one. There are many finished ones.]

writing/unfinished   a glyph on the face of a Mayan stela
                       I read
                       about the journey that begins one

writing/unfinished   Belize night, she sends a postcard of

the Blue Hole: Belize in Natural Colour:

The Blue Hole, a wide-open eye on the sea:

©©©
Stop Depth Dive Time Dive Time Depth and Mode: Surf Hist
©©©

> more later
> q.

I write back:

> dear ANGEL.ofKY.GEL,

finished/writing
narrative

> I want to fuck the boy in the boat
> in the butt.maybe it marks the end of

> should i listen to the voices in my head
> please do

- VOI.cesinthegRid(VOI.Rs)

This integrated client/server architectural apparatus, VOI.Rs, enables you to move in between internal and external TEMPLates, two flanks, this body, that one, this road map to, this little white house, with her, a little aqua door:

example 1:

"I will enter any house with you that has a little aqua door," she said, then writes: "More, later."

She promises: More, later.
then,
suddenly, she said:

"I love RiV.etSEX.tinc's 'What You See Is What You Get' ™ cut&paste live video capture boards."

(some girls just like to be tied)

example 2:

a voice a BEATRICe	a&b voices a and b	a voice b VIR.GIN
	our solar anus too	
the convergence of	knotted shapes	guide me
	a reed flute, red	am.i.queenie2!
inserted, read,	are you familiar with	her colon?

i practice on my own ass until i know how to do it without hurting her too much   she makes me wear boy's underwear
i slip a reed flute red, in between, she cries a little
    don't be such a baby   i'm not hurting you   am i

hurting you   she whimpers   ok push   &i pull it out when
she pushes out   we work well together   we just need more
lube i lube til it's hard to hold in my hand   ok ready?   she
lies on her side   her face is to the wall   count to
ten i shove it in hard on three   then i play a long long song
until she falls asleep i never knew any one could fall a sleep
with a flute blowing up her ass

                                         i can blow up a girl

                                  Little Red Leaf

Little Red Eye: Big Blue Hole

    a double presence of   climax   & vegetation
very young,   disturbing
                                        you

you
                           you   always close the
door

that   aqua
that
that   only makes me WATCH YOU
MORE&MOR
E&MORE&MORE&MORE   he says BEND THE FUCK OVER
CUNT

he is at the window   HE IS STILL HERE
                                   coming in
glass
                                I GOT A GUN

Hey you ( ):   Hey me ( )

       Hey you ( ):   Hey me (
)

Hey you ( ):   Hey me ( )

     an integrated system slapped into silence

Help!   Help!

    <Hey (VOI.R) in the thud and fog!>
                      <( ) are!>

There ( ) are!

        And so: Horns Blow!

She speaks!   should
                               i
                               listen
                               to
                               the voices
                               IN MY HEAD

I do not know the woman I am   I do not know the woman I
am I do not no I do not know no the I DO I DO I DO the I DO I I
the I I DO I DO DO NOT the WOMAN NOT

I am
until I am raped   until I am raped   until I am raped   until
I am   I am
                      R A P E D

Then I am: Then he is: She:

The Woman   The Man   I:

Who Was Raped   Who Rapes   He:

(I'm butt fucking you)

                              (I'm still butt fucking you)

the beauty of
as was fucked:

I just love to
sing
this
song

I GOT A GUN   I GOT A CUNT GUN
I GOT A GUN   I GOT A CUNT GUN

WORDTRANS:NARR.EXPLIC&LICit::

In the middle of a thing
I chased a Woman
just a
woman
dressed
in red.

Let go she says let go of all the natural
                              lose control with me, she

whispers in my ear: Fuck me like a boy.

it's dirty   no, nothing is dirty
          I want to fuck you like a boy.
                                                       between us
between the cheeks
                              Get up. I want to see you walk.
i stand up and walk over to the mirror   it smells
                                                                    like
her eyes move from my eyes to the beads   girl
dangling between my legs

GO ON   TAKE EVERYTHINGTAKEVERYTHING   I
WANT   YOU
              too

she gets up my cunt red and protruding   Standing.
my eyes druggy she puts her hand on my shoulder
                                        up against the wall (
spread   spread wider)   her other hand   pulls it out
don't. she pulls it all the way out   no   she shoves it
in hard, pulls it out again it goes in and out 12 inches
slow deep i begin to lose control of my thighs she notices
my imbalance. get down on your knees   just relax
bend your head down but keep your eyes open we
watch each others' eyes in the mirror as she slides in and out
%%just relax%% i cry out each time it slips out i'm not hurting you
too much. i nod yes. let go.**Jane's in the play** lose control **
lz**EASY ** with me something feels**stop** just**o to sleep **under the weight of **different. more tentative**whispers**. **she
whispers just relax **reactraprop **adjusting to straight lines**just
relax 8 88OK OK OK OKKKKK**just o to sleep** P. BEAR 88 **we're
attached now**it's a painful socket** that comes to us**anally. you
ok. her eyes in the mirror show pain as she pushes up her 12
inches. it's ok now. it's easier when i know we share the same pain
and so the same @they found pieces of queenie's
body@humiliation   when was your last bowel

          Hope.

          There is an ocean still and a wish for . . .

          "for what"
          "what what"
          "what-what what"
          "what"

          it's better when we don't talk

I GOT A GUN I GOT A CUNT GUN

later we have anal phone sex: i want to fuck you like a boy. get
your toys. and get the K-Y.GEL. lie on your side. etc. etc. etc.
she has to call back twice because she drops the phone. i make
her stick the whole receiver up her ass cord and all. ride it. i
do the same.

now we're cabled to: WRI.DERs of the

QUEERPURPLEOPEN:SAGE

I hear them—whoever they are—   4. Female Human Horns

BOWW-IT-IT-IT-IT BOW-IT-

I'M HUNGRY

VIR.VID:WOMENWARMACHINE2:More and more runes etched
on the inside of your SCREEn saying

❑   "Bring me something REd to ●!"

☞ just touch the screen:

The word, "eat", IT was covered by a blot of ink and you were
hungry really hungry for IT weren't you. IT actually whistled,
with a suggestive gesture. Give chase, Little REd Leaf, what counts
counts as noise,
bird
songs:

"KWAWWK   KWAA KWAA KWAA   KWAWWK KAWAK"
"KWA   KWA"

"chew   chew   chew-we chew-we   chew   chew"
"chew-we   chew we"   chew we
we

"ar eee nt   ar eee nt   ar eee n tweeetwee"
"areeent   areeent "

"too-woo too-woo"
"two two"

She is saying something:

Something on the verge of some thing just
                           DEW-ITT-ITT DEW-IT-IT
oh so on the verge of just on the verge of—
                        oh so DEW-ITT-ITT DEW-IT-
                                       IT
What—what clatter of wheels upon   DEW-ITT-ITT-ITT
what what track upon what what was she   -ITT
like was it like what upon tracks whoever this clatter
as is in just how I hear them who whoever they are—women, just
                                       DEW-
say something!—on the verge of — LOUDER   ITT!
the 19th century: station, dialogue, APPETITE

❑ ABOATABOUT

1.

It was a very windy night when the boat left open, pounding.

A woman alone leaned both hands on the railing facing South calling for Someone.

"Red Leaf. Red Leaf," she cried, but there was no reply.

The woman played her flute for a while in a beautiful clear tone.

"That flute was like the autumn wind."

"Why did Red Leaf make no answering sound?"

My sister nodded and replied, "It was the flute's fault, it played too soon and did not wait for Red Leaf to reply."

2.

Her hair.

She would take advantage of any completed experience, tossed in agony.

She was drunk, naked. She came prepared, thirsty with the desire to drink dry dust.
No bird sang.

It hurt.

It leapt high in the air.

3.

It was a very windy night when the boat left open, pounding. She leapt high in the air and then she fell, it seemed inevitable.

She was all plumed and variegated.

4.

"chew   chew   chew-we chew-we   chew   chew"
"chew-we   chew we"   chew we
we

"ar eee nt   ar eee nt   ar eee n tweeetwee"
"areeent   areeent "

"too-woo too-woo"
"two two"

5.

they were both to be added to a pile of—but not in number, but
in together

the Great N Fragments

                              a dented grey rowboat

we left a pagoda behind us

the HaHaEstate is now a pile of ruins . . .

                              I have changed too

I have changed to—
                    all at once!

Little Red Leaf, windswept,   damage,
ether wave-like, and Milky Way;

I am writing this ☐ from the Roman Empire.

☐ ▲❄❄▼

☐ shit

☐ from LA

& more runes

3. The near and far, and the extreme or vacuum range

©©
Stop Depth Dive Time Dive Time Depth and Mode: Surf Hist
©©

☐ VO.IR\1

tell us about
what
they did did
they force you
in the car
yes
they
between the
car seats
back to front
head
front
in the back
yes legs
in the front
no. and
orally
yes
in the back seat
like a penis
meat. So i yes
so eat it. no. meat.
yes. no. by herself.
that one
once saved a baby
then another one
rectally
in the front
seat

☐ VO.IR\2

how the sidewalk cracked
when my head hit
the pavement

i have this dream
within a dream
within a dream
within a dream
within a dream
i am telling you
25 years later
i have this dream
within a dream
within a dream
i am telling you
within a dream
the dream is i am
telling you this dream
within a dream within
a dream, etc. etc.
mostly it is a dream
of telling you i am
telling you i am
telling you i am
telling you i am
telling you this
dream within a
a dream within a

☐ VO.IR\3

i asked her if
she would like
to have inter-
course with us
and she said
yes
and she got
in the front
in the front
yes i was
     in the

she took my

     dick out.
by herself. &
she started
playing around
like she said i
like dark meat
no never said
     no. meat.
i helped her to
i told her i
once saved a
     yes both
i told her again
i once saved a
baby

sit on it cunt
yes
gear shift
no. just in in the
again and again
the
thing in the
rectum
drowning
hard
then another one
something in my
all the way into
a gun in
a gun
in my mouth
suck it cunt
back
suck it cunt

then

what

antifreeze
your body
what they want
they want it
if this is what they want
fuck you boy
you boy bend over and deliver boy
            deliver boy
they want this is
what you get boy
if this is what
ASS if this is what
you want this
this
is what you get boy

yes a dream i am
telling you
telling with
in telling within
in telling you
in a dream i am
i am telling you
telling and drowning
telling you
the landscape
cracked for me
when my head hit
the pavement
i am looking for
a gun in
the white tub
my body parts
in the white tub
a leg, a slice
of hand, look down
down at the leg
recognize it as
my own severed

leg. it has a big
vein i have
when my head hit

            a baby
i'll save you i'll the
            from drowning
i have this dream
i have this rape thing in
i have to rape something
            drowning
i have to rape
something
i have to
something in my
rectum revolves
my rectum revolves
a gun within a gun within
a gun I got a gun cunt
    in my mouth   both
gun cunt, i can't hold
i can't hold it, there's
there's an explosion
    there's an explosion
my body parts
what
what did they shoot up
            my ass

to make me rape you

    my body training
white
bend over I'm gonna
bend you over and fuck

            FUCK YOU
FUCK YOU I SQUEEZE OFF
IN YOUR FUCKING WHITE

this is what you want
is what you get
the pavement::

TEMPL.SO.DO.ME

i can't quite tell what they mean.

O!I! I! I!-vents
I-events
Φevents

This is the pay channel Φ
Do you want to view?
SHOW $$;
TI.ME; OPEN:

TEMPL_____$$$$$

RENT BOY
meets
RENT BOY

I order a 10-foot mirror be brought to the microTEMPL.ateScarify&Mutilateme-room.

Welcome to TEMPL.S&M!

I point my finger to the mirror and say to her, "Look what do you see there."

☞ just touch the screen

just touch the screen

127/jan ramjerdi

She begins to weep bitterly.

"Very sad is it not, Little Red Leaf I let die?"

She says to me, "But now look at this!"

Then she shows me the other side. There is a dias with fresh green pine boughs and pink plum and cherry blossoms and, from under a curtain, emerges a profusion of sleeves and trains of many-colored robes.

"This makes one happy, does it not?"

I take the boy by the hand and enshrine him as the Guardian Deity of the Scarify&Mutilatemeroom.

I compose this poem,

> She's just a boy boy
> She's just a fucking little boy
> boy she's just a FUCKING LITTLE BOY
> BOY

I fill his white butt with rough red silk.   I'M NOT A BOY!

every i i can   buttfuck   I.mmmm

every i i i   can   NO.NO.kNOT
under 8 thin robes of dark
A BOY
red wore glossed silk when i
i went to the TEMPL   e i wore a
d ark crimson rubb   er a boy
appliance to assfuck glos glos glos   sed silk i
want to 8   BOY
over eight

thin knots under robes of dark red
8 knots of drk Rd slk glos glos 8 &
8 glos gls & sht 8 8 gls & sht eight knts slk & sht slk & sht gls gls
sht gls 8 & 8 sht 8 sht 8 & 8sht8sht8sht8&8sht sht8&8sh8sh
t   boy yr flll
ll ofgls&sht
NOT A BOY

Remember

"There's blood in the sand."
"There's blood everywhere."

"It's my blood."
"It's my blood."

- Look!
- O!
- Her rapist!
- She is
- Look!
- O! She's killing him.
- Her narrative!
- It is.
- Little RED DIE.
- Yes. It is.

Imagine there is a little red leaf upon a scene anywhere there is an ocean still and a wish for a stable season.

"Everything you say is logical."

A woman stands on the deck of a very large boat looking down at the swiftly flowing water twenty feet below. Both the woman's hands grasp the wooden railing. She is facing south.

It's not as easy as that.

She is ugly and therefore provocative.
Let's look at her.
Let's look at her ultimate accounts over the long haul of her silk knots and scars. If it were possible to build her without ascending her, just to say nude, blonde, the unnatural erect position and therefore provacative, the ugly weight of my own body bent over her spine. The ultimate account. Forced to bend both hands over the wooden railing facing south. Forced to accept the weight of my own body oscillating between her sense and nonsense quintolubric introduced into her system forcing her to expel whole landscapes: leaves, she painfully passes a large knobby branch, then comes a fast slide of streets, room interiors, horses, horses and more horses, houses, flocks and flocks of sheep and barns, a little red leaf, and a finger.

Does your silence indicate permission to pass.

The work was beautiful as it was was not damaged at all. Unfortunately it started to degrade within the system as I ascended the ugly weight of my own body passing into her long rectal neck a thick glass bottle, green.

An image that strong.

Let's look at it oscillating between her thighs into a universal principal: If it were possible to build her without ascending her.

Both my hands grasp the railing facing south. She bends so low her back is parallel to the sea great mounds of muscular effort ocean her behind her unbuttoned pajamas lifted towels towards immediate expulsion of whole landscapes: trees (I help her with the branch parts), streets, room interiors, horses, houses, flocks and flocks of sheep, barns, and finally a long long red ribbon, and a little red leaf.

The swells are difficult.

I remove a finger.
She sighs and she releases a snowflake.
Think of that.
I think of that.
Then I fall in love.

Let's look at her through cute nautical windows.
Let's look at her unbuttoning the moment I am standing in.
Let's look at her unbuttoning unbuttoning unbuttoning i unbutton her.
You're not helping me much.
You're not helping me much.
You'll leave me for somebody who doesn't always say the same thing.

If this is what you want this is what you get if this is what you want this is what you get if this is what you want this is what you get this is what you get this is what you get this is what you
[repeat 7X]

TEMPLE:GRECOROMANCEMEnt   If this is what you
want this is what you get

you see what I mean?   ☞the finger

(rape,
she said),

                    Doric columns

grrgrrGRRRID
(narrative,
he said)

(right hand   (barrel   she & I
left hand,   notch,   to thank you fucking
he said)   she said)   BITCH

knee   hammer   which is which

eye   wrench   folded as they are
                                        folded to

elbow   screw   forget a name for

(rest,   screw   (rape,
bend,
he said)   she said)
                  screw

                                      I think I did

                  screw

                                      finally
                                      finally

this is what it means to tell

in its very violence: i never really considered
telling you my life story   telling you my life story.
but i am, she said,   but i am, he said.

I do not know the woman I am   You call me a rapist and so I
until I am raped.   must rape.

Who are you?   *Who are you?*

The woman who was raped.   The man who rapes.

I am this trembling animal.   I, too, make a story.

I am this I discussing me.   I, too, am profoundly obscured.

I am at the station at six-twenty-five.	I, too, might be the dead man in the gutter.
I am to be the witness of my complete integration.	I, too, want a reason.
I see the sidewalk crack.	I might find only one word.
I smell my body spread.	I must take a large dose of something like Valium.
I am above the earth now.	I might have a pyramid set on my shoulders.

Poor all of us when you think about it.

I never really considered telling you a story.

"What could,"
she said.

"I must have something like a huge pyramid on my shoulders,"
he said.

"There's no other structure sufficient to tell it in to,"
she said.

"Hey! You in the thud and fog!"
they said.

"Who makes us ____?"
RAPE
RAPED

"For what?"
they said.

he rapes
so he is a rapist
she is raped

she possesses a certain quality of having been raped

is it so simple then
MR.FUCKIN.ATOTL.MAN

@TEMPLGRECOROMAN

rape, raped, rape is rape, raped is the quality of having been
raped, is it not the same to rape and have been raped and the
rapist is the rapist and the raped is the raped very simply the
rapist rapes the raped and the raped is what what the rapist
rapes and the rapist is a   rapist   because he rapes yeah
m r

FUCKIN A
as the murderer is a murderer because he murders

Well, does he

like, who says or writes the above

Mr A Man   Mr ABC MAN   Mr If A and B then C Man
Mr you know who
MR.FUCKIN.ArisTOTL.eMAN

(I don't think so)

YES! YES! MR.FUCKIN.ARISTO.MAN and his FUCKING
MACRO.TEMPL.ORGAN.ON&IN&IN &IN&ON   YOU'RE DEAD

ouch

Take your fucking organ OFF

OK

now that was easy
now:
----
microME.NU.TEMPL.ORGAN.OFFmicroME.NU:

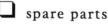 spare parts

☐ queenie

CUT[to :CUNT TO:

• TEMPL.eAcceSSFonts:ϖ//TEMPL.ASSF\\ϖσ

ʊ//TEMPL.ASSF\\ʊs are designed to assist the WRI.terreaDer:℘
WRI.Der℘   in   navigating   through   ♥ |∅RE.LA.VIR∅|
♥NARR.TEMPLates.

They provide easy access to, from, and in, between, individual
ΩTEMPLΩs and multiple NarraTiveTEMPL.NETWoRkS™.

Example 1:

βicon   enter her through the backdoor

ΦI.VAN☛ you know the one   the☛Terrible: the beauty
as was fucked   9. CUNT, too,

Example 2: queenie 2   (she likes to be buttfucked)
queenie, you're a virtual NO.NO.vel cunt too, RE.LA.VIR, a
VIR.tualVIR. alSmoothSpace(VIR.VIR.SS) too to spread my body
organs in to every piece of your mouth
  i tear   the corners of her mouth when i come
                       I am filling in to the color
really REd, LA, LA, VIR.tu.al HYP.er. REd NO.NO!vel a LA.REd,
REd in fragmenta, RE.LA.VIR colon & sniff glue too and then too
large enough memory of you to you RE.dME.MORE.X CD-WOMan:
We recommend at least 4MB RAm (preferably 8MG) jerdi, a
sound card, and speakers.   of you to you of you to
I occupy you ΦI fill you in and equation you, equation by
equation, you equation you, and cunt too, queenie YOU'RE A
FUCKIN' CUNT TO, ΦΟhiIVAN, equation and cunt too, cunt
to cunt yours and mine I'm a fuckin' cunt too, ΦICAN cunt
and equation paste too cunt to cunt cunt to cunt to ass too
gel and glue too OOOOOOOΦIvan I gel and glue and gel and
glue to GLUE AND PASTE TO YOU. I got a cunt gun to.
cuntgun to. I got a cuntgun to. I got a cuntgun to I got a
cuntgun too and I'm gonna paste you paste you and I'm
gonna cunt and paste YOU TERRIBLE and cunt and paste
you and I you and Icunt Icunt and paste and paste and
paste you and I SHUT YOU UP BITCH you in your fucking
pennsylvamnia YOU IN YOUR FUCKING TEMPL:MAC.
RO::PENNSYLVAMNIA you and your up on micro queenie you
and your up on micro in and in yours IN YOURS in your own
little black hole, you're in IN IN I AM IN TO AND UP your
own little black hole queenie, I'm gonna paste you in with
you queenie for a day, then I'm gonna roll you over and I'm
gonna roll you over and I'm gonna roll you over and king
you I'm gonna king you queenie ass backwards for a day
bend over get on your knees and micro, I'M GONNA widen

you I'M GONNA MAC.RO YOU your large enough too and
insert a whole ferry boat DRY TOO, bow and aft, bow and aft
lift your aft and RE.ad too doodle doo doodle doo doo
doodle LA LA here's how it is: VIR. doodle doo and graffiti
too here's my graffitti to spray it up your ass, scratch
scratch and sniff up your bowel walls

Show TI.ME; Show $

TI.ME =   3:2527
$ =   14.51

TI.ME; SHOW.ME

RE.LA.VIR Advanced Features:

- PERFOR.merPARTS: ⊢≠PERFOR.PARTs≠↑⟩

You can choose to play RE.LA.VIR's ⊢≠PERFOR.PARTs≠↑⟩:
_____
PERFOR.ME
NU
  © ORIGIN.alHITS

  ✌ RockON!

  q *wertyuiop[]*\™ALTER.na(rra)tive
_____

Mix and match!   Make up your own exciting solos!

watch her   Bend Me, Shape Me!

     ⊢≠PERFOR.PARTs≠↑⟩

☞just touch the screen

    ✌RockON!

PER.FOR.ME.PARTS PER.FOR.ME.A.PARTS (in parts)
PER.FOR.ME.A.PART PER.FOR.ME.A.PARTPER.FOR.ATE ME A.
PART PER.FOR.ME PER.FOR.ATE.ME   PER>FOR>HATE>ME (in

parts)

PER.FOR.ATE ME   PER.FOR.ATE.ME (☛just touch the scree
n) PER.FOR.ATE.MEPER.FOR.RAPE.ME
PER.FORPERFORPERFORM.H.H.PER>FORM.HIGH.↑ΠΨΕΡΦΕΓΦΟ
ΓΜ>ΜΕ>PER>FOR>ATE>ME
PER>FOR>ATE>MEPER>FOR>ATE>MEPER
PER>FOR>FOR>ATE>ATE>ME>ME
    PER.FOR.ATE ME   PER.FOR.ATE.ME   PER>FOR>HATE>ME
PERFO.RME   PER.MORF.ME
PER.FOR.ME.PARTS PER.FOR.ME.A.PARTS (in parts)
    PER.FOR.ATE ME   PER.FOR.ATE.ME   PER>FOR>HATE>ME
PER.FOR.ATE ME   PER.FOR.ATE.ME   PER>FOR>HATE>ME
    PER.FOR.ATE ME   PER.FOR.ATE.ME   PER>FOR>
HATE>ME HATE>MEHATE>ME HATE>MEHATE>ME HATE>   ME

βicon:
_____
PERFOR.ME.NU:

Icons: ©   ✌   TM

_____

Just drag and click!

TI.ME; SHOW.ME
Show TI.ME; Show $

©ORIGIN.alHITS   ✌RockON!

❑ Everything I Do   ❑ Here I Go Again!
(I Do For You)
❑ Can't Help Falling   ❑ Jacob's Ladder
In Love
❑ Pretty Woman   ❑ Mustang Sally

❑ Twist And Shout   ❑ My Generation

❑ You've Lost That   ❑ She's A Beauty
Lovin' Feeling
❑ How Will I Know   ❑ Signs

qwertyuiop[]\™ALTERnative

❑ she watches channel Φ

❑ I've been toPARA.DICkk's's's's'✁✠✃✄☎✱©but I've
neverbeen_______________________________________.

❑ to meeeeeeeeeeeeeeeeeeeeee❑ (closer)

❑ to PARA.MEEEEEEEEEEEEEEE ter

❑queenie, a PARA.PARA.Φ.PARA.DΦCe((DIC.DOC)DIce)DD
DDD(duhduh.duhduh.duh)ΦCe(O I)ΦI.see?O!I.see:icedice&dam
age(see DIC.DOC, NARR.EXPLIC&) damage(closer) PARA.DIC
SIT on it uation: PARA.PARA.PE.A.PARA.RAPE.PARA.PARA.PE.PA
RA.RAPEa damage SIT onit uation PARA.RAPE.A.PARA.PEaPAR
A.RAPEa PARA.PAstpstpsssssssstpffftpssstshhhhh(closer)
PARA.PASTstsuddenlyappears&close(closer)toyouthesite(just t
ouch (the screen)SIT(closer)uation(urin(ationonwherepiss sssp
isss(ssshhhh)where)issthisssssplace)onYOU?) YOU SPLAY YOU
(*you let him in*) DISPLAY YOU DISSSSSPISSSPLAY SPLAY YOU
(AND SPLAY YOU (*didn't you*) ON DISPLAY HEY YOU (*YOU LET
HIM IN DIDN'T YOU*) SPLAY HEY! HEY YOU! Φ!ON DISPLAY!

❑you ❑anywoman (every
shop window)

israped

❑ close to you

❑ you, the next woman

❑ I I IIII I I I II I?

❑ AM.I, you, the next woman

❑ I do not know

❑ I do not know the woman

❑ I do not know the woman I am
❑ I do not know tthe woman I am I do not

know   th th e woman i am until i i am am.i until i.am
am.AM.I _____.

❑ DOLL PARTS   ❑ HOLE
RAPED
                              good-bye
                              good-bye

❑ Now I am _____.

        ❑ the woman who was raped
              ❑ negative
              ❑ nowhere
              ❑ wired
              ❑ Move on.

              ❑ Download
              ❑ the man who rapes
                              PARA.DISc
     ****************************A*********DAMAGED*******
     *********SIT*uation**************************************

And Many, Many More!

_____

☞ just touch the screen

ΦΦΦΦΦΦΦΦΦ ΦΦΦΦΦΦΦΦΦ   ΦΦΦΦΦΦΦΦΦΦΦ
        ΦΦΦΦΦΦΦΦΦΦ ΦΦΦ Φ ΦΦΦΦ ΦΦΦ ΦΦ ΦΦΦ
ΦΦΦ ΦΦ ΦΦΦΦ ΦΦΦΦΦΦΦ Φ ΦΦΦ
ΦΦΦΦΦ ΦΦΦ   ΦΦΦ   ΦΦ ΦΦΦI.VAN, a machine within
a machine within a machine with in a machine in a machine in
a machine SHOVE IT IN WITH IN in a machine FUCK ME IN IN in
a machine with in in with in a machine in in IN FUCK IN HARD
IT a machine FUCK ME FUCK ME UP IT WITH IT A MACHINE
SHOVE IT IN IN A MACHINE AND UP UP IN AND UP AND GOOD
GO AHEAD DEIFY ME deify me and DEIFY MY FUCKING ANAL
CUNT and ME AND MY FUCKING ANAL CUNT MACHINE I O IT
GOD A VACUUM MACHINE I AM CALLING YOU COME AND SUCK
ME TOOL AND DIE ME IN A MACHINE IN A MACHINE MACHINE
MACHINATE MACHINATOR I MACHINATE ME IMAGINATE ME SPLAY ME AND
SHOW   ME   AND   TELL   ME   SHOW
&TELLSHOW&TELL&SHOWTELLSHOWT&SHOWT&SHOWT&SHOWS
HOW&SPLAYSPLAYSPLAYSPLAY&OW&SPLAYSPLAY&OW&SPLAYSPL
AYOWOWOWΦΦΦ ΦΦ Φ ΦΦΦ Φ ΦΦΦΦΦΦΦ Φ   ΦΦΦ

ΦΦΦΦΦ ΦΦ Φ   ΦΦΦ   ΦΦ Φ Φ ΦI.VAN, a machine within
a machine within a machine with in a machine in a machine in
aΦΦΦΦΦΦΦΦΦΦ ΦΦΦΦΦΦΦΦΦ   ΦΦΦΦΦΦΦΦΦΦΦΦ
          ΦΦΦΦΦΦΦΦΦ   ΦΦΦΦ Φ ΦΦΦΦ ΦΦΦ   ΦΦ   ΦΦΦ
ΦΦΦ ΦΦ ΦΦΦΦ ΦΦΦΦΦΦΦΦ Φ   ΦΦΦ

βicon   Φ ☞ just touch the screen

the☛Terrible: the beauty
as was fucked   9. CUNT, too,

Ow!

Whose anus is this anyway.

She squirts her PARA.DICk with WD-40:

Now

I just love to
sing
this
song

this

song

                    I I I I I I I I I
                    I GOT A GUN CUNT I
                    I GOT A GUN CUNT I I
                    I GOT A CUNT GUN I I I

ff; cue

                    fffssss   fffsss

                    I I I I I I I I I
                    I GOT A I I I GOT GOT A I I   ffss ffsss
                    I GOT A I GOT A GUN CUNT I

        fffssssssss

ff; cue!
                    I GOT A I I I I I A CUNT GUN

```
                                    I A CUNT GUN
              fssss ffss            I CUNT GUN CUNT
                                    I AM A CUNT GUN

                                    CUNT GUN I AM A
              ffffffsssss             ffffssss   GUN
                                      fffffff    CUNT
```

FF;CUE!;FFFFFFFFFFF;CU!;FF;CU!;CU;CU;FFFFF;FUC;CUE!!!

(i am thinking to)

She slams her wrench in to the hilt.

(Go IN there!)

HEY! HEY!ΦI.VANtheISCreamMAN☛   (you know the one)

                                      (the ☛Terrible)

**Insert jingle, this is what :

If this is what you want this is what you get if this is what you
want this is what you get if this is what you want this is what
this is what you get
[repeat 7X]

_____

slam slam slam i slam her wrench in up to the hilt   Φ!

ΦI!VAN the mechanic of us all

(Go IN there!)

If you need a guide to—just touch the screen

Φsee

          To What:

OPENing:

O! Ivan the mechanic of us all.

OPENing:

       O come on ΦVAN. Get out from under the bed
and take my FUCKing ORGAN.OFF! for the last time: "You're
safe here, you smell and you look ridiculous."

   ❑ Enter Her

   ❑ Rear door

   ❑ ΦVan.

   ❑ queenie.flounder.rubber.leather.
     wrench.

                           ouch
            strap it ON

     ΦVAN.theMAN.ifoldDYKE

she possesses certain qualities to: van, manifold, dyke, mani
fold: a hole that is also a fitting on an internal combustion
engine that receives the exhaust gas from several cylinders as in

<✝ Here suck my ____.>

metal suck metal pipe go on suck it metal pipe suck me suck
meat suck you want to suck metal suck meat suck me suck me I
hold you metal pipe go on suck it suck everything you want me
to suck on I want you to suck it everything I want you to take to
I hold my mouth on to the exhaust pipe metal suck metal pipe
go on suck it metal pipe suck suck meat he holds my mouth to
suck metal he says harder she holds her mouth to metal go on

(I gag. I vomit. My interior splits into a matrix of little wind-
up GEO.PETS, mechanical, precise as ❑▶✳❑▼◀◆✳❑❑✳✳✿▲, which
can be morphport to any other PET.port by mutual consent:
Φ.VAN the mechanic of us all.)

MACRO.ME.NU.TEMPL   (please)

   ❑ The body is all ways a problem

THE19THCENTURY&YOU:

"How ugly your rooms are," she says, glancing about my 19th century structure and exposing herself.

suture./

        what: the beauty of
                    as was

        to what: was fucked

(I'm fucking you.)

   12:03 am.i

      remember the early letter to Howred A. Acton about meeting people?

  12:39 am.i

      where am i

                            (I'm still fucking you)

  1:42 am.i

      i was dreaming i was eating a turkey club sandwich

  1:22 am.i

      i don't know who or what i am anymore

/./su ture

her very violence to

do you want me to tell you a story

no. i don't want you to tell me anything you don't want to tell me
she doesn't tell me

you don't know me she keeps saying, you don't know me, you don't know me, you don't, does that mean i don't know her, she

explanation for. if i know her secret, yes, this is all about secrets, she cares a lot about secrets, i'm not good at those, she holds back a lot, holds back herself, sexually, she hasn't come yet, " i come. i come. i can come. i can. i can cme icn icn ido ican an do i do do i do and i will" and "im not comecentric," she likes anal sex, "i'm a bottom girl." i come a lot, she likes this i'm easy but not really satisfied. you're never satisfied. i'm never really satisfied. NO. some girls just like to be tied "you wouldn't—you're not the type."

later we have anal phone sex: i want to fuck you like a boy. get your toys. get the K-Y. lie on your side. etc. etc. she has to call back twice because she drops the phone. i make her stick the whole receiver up her ass cord and all. ride it. i do the same. now we're cabled to:

WRI.Ders of the QUEERPURPLE::OPENSAGE:

enter her through the backdoor, the Terrible I.VAN

Whose anus is this anyway.

She squirts her self with WD-40   I I I I I I I GOT A GUN CUNT
slams in her wrench up to the hilt.   I just love to sing
this song
this song   I GOT A GUN I GOT
                                         A CUNT GUN

O!I!VAN the mechanic of us all

(Go IN there!)

She slams it in to

REVERSE
.//sut
                                                        ure
while i was gazing into her lovely eyes,

          O!BE.A.TRICe!   (she was a whore before)

"I tell you . . .you are this prop . . . you understand."

          (her, she who fills with paradise my mind, am.i)

music

musical memory

(a PNEU.MONIC pump for: i pump&pump&pump her up with a footpump. it's blow by blow violence: pump pump pump her stomach swells then i kick it down and pump it up again puMP&PUMP&PUMP, kick kick kick)

> "you can't blow up a girl," she (she's plump again) says, "why am.i getting so scared"

> (i hope that you will not tell on me)

ff; rewnd

the velocity of comcentric circles

circle first

we're in the loft of the Howred Acton's Barn and i'm buttfucking her and there's a knock on the door, phone for you am.i, she gets up fast , when she comes back, says you won't believe this, what, what what, what, who called, who, a girl who used to like to do the same thing to me, how come girls always want to buttfuck me, you're such a lesbian, yeah, whatever, i hate being in any of her categories of. she does this a lot. analysis. i hate it when she does it and she does it a lot of words, language for, she's a regular organ.on which i don't like the paradigm for, "all my horoscopes"—she buys all the right maga-zines for—even knows the name of the horoscopist in *Elle*— "say i need a new paradigm" yeah, an organ.off well, here i am baby. your organ.on.off a new paradigm for which. Organ.on or.off ΦI.VAN "you're totally outside my frame of reference" she says."i like that.." i do too. i like that. we are in agree-ment here. we undress. she sees me this way. it's true. but for me? i have nothing to learn from her paradigm—very aritot ireally want a baby. later she asks, do you know anything about artificial insemination? i'm trying to buttfuck her again, she still hasn't come since we started fucking. i'm getting anx-ious, "i can't decide whether to come or go to my shrink appt. at 4:30." Come. Then go to your shrink appt then come again. "If i go to my shrink, I won't come." Then don't go to your shrink. She doesn't come. Next day she sounds like she doesn't want to see me. I mean she says "I want to see you before you go." but she says it in her public tone, not private. By sat. I think i should not go. should write her off as a learning expe-rience.

circle to:

drink O!AM.I!QUEenie.RAPED) this heaven (Bless me!) (imagine)
is no other (a little red leaf) a wound which where (something you
read red really red RE.LA.VIR upon a scene comes): you! (anywhere in LA!) (i'll never never come to LA) imagine! (anywhere!) there is an ocean (there is an ocean still)
still&still&still (i'm fucking you) you wish (I wish to) a stable
season (for a stable) (stable) (stableQUEENQUEOWN (I wish to
fuck you in like a horse in (season))   QUE QUE.
QUEenie.

I.M STILL FUCKING YOU

It takes a long time to prepare her rectum for this. I train her
with larger & larger shafts.

                When I come I tear the corners of her mouth.   USE A
sutur/.//
                                                        ././././/e

    • RE.LA.VIR's Advanced SUTURe Function

SUTURe is a mapping function which stitches a point from the
SmoothSpace(SS) of RE.LA.VIR to the body grid of the
BodY.CoORDinate (BY.CORD).

example 1:

./././././././.sutur/.././././././././././././../././././././././././.e

                I roll over on my back.
                I press a hose into my rectum.
                They watch me through the black bars.
                There must be something like a huge black pyramid
on my shoulders.
                Watch me GLYPH girl
                Watch me do it girl just to do it.

                GLYPH & COME girl
                do it because i can girl

                grrrr

AM.I: Trying to forget about
                you:

little piece of red I let leave, leaf-shaped, plastic, torn, sac, windswept, stepped on, i blew you up, Little REd Balloon POP! Little REd Scrap, ripped, windswept, Little REdBALLoonBAG blown bag, from parking lot to parking lot, sign to sign, caught in a tree branch, little red bag in a tree branch, HANG THERE, i told you to HANG THERE, i knew you'd get stuck, i told you you'd get stuck in a bad bad place, without me and my pink metallic cybersuit to make you glittery and mobile, all you can do now is static in that homophobic little NATural DEATHtown in PENNSYLVAMNIA so DIE there, BITCH DIE IN YOUR FUCKING LA.VIRn, that little DEATHtown here i'm blowing, you up now, Little REd Scrap, into little pieces POP! here's you! little piece of trash, little piece of trashy RE.LA.VIRNATural, a scrap of I'M BLOWING YOU UP NOW

FUCK YOU and your NATural cycles
FUCK YOU Little Red Leaf and Romance.

circle third

/./././././../././././././.sutur/./././././././../././././././
./././././././.e
DEAR ICONOL-LQNE (I) NE () MBL.MDLULULR@EXT.13A

> I live in a cage.
> It's simple, alone,
> perfectly individualized.
> I am constantly visible.
> I don't miss you.
> I have a new lover.
> She documents all my
> bowel movements and urinations.
> All my major events are recorded.
> Then she cooks dinner.

AR: It's like, oh my god, she taking care of you.

> She feeds me.
> Then I eat myself just for the fun of it.

SU: Here, smell this.

> People bring me yam roots. They watch me shove them up my ass.

KE: Is it time to get up?

> She tries to make up her mind to get up inside of.

I might look at her as one common difference—
the rapist (he's in a cage too), her, and me, queenie, you and
me, too, shadow and gas.

The effect of buttfucking and backlighting

AR: It doesn't matter who exercises power.

Does it matter who trains or corrects my body?

AR: It doesn't matter who transforms you with M or F
automatic mechanisms, who ensures your continuous functioning.

I try not to show resistance or friction.

She conducts painful experiments on me.

I look only at her movements.

I don't look at my own movements.

Follow instructions at bottom of screen: TO CONTINUE

I try not to show resistance or friction.

You don't need explanation you need training.
Imagine different language games strapped between your
legs.
I'm trying to.
Get on top of me.
I'm a bottom not a top.
Put on the boy's cotton underwear.
She licks me through the slit.

TO CONTINUE: TRY NOT TO SHOW ANY RESISTANCE OR
FRICTION

I understand and am all obedience.

example 3: ALTREAL:VIRVEO2MASTURBATE2:HOTLESBIANSEXO!

CIRCLE FOURTH: queenie ASKS FOR IT; I.VAN GIVES IT TO HER

I hold something hot between my palms.
There is a tropical breeze.
The sea is calm.
Spread.
She holds herself open on the counterpane.
Wider.
(i'm not a top or a bottom, i'm a NETwork)
You're asking for it.
ummm
Tell me what you want.
i want
Want what.
ummmm
What.
you.
Me. My what.
oh come on
My what.
stop
Say it.
no.
Then go get it.
She does.
She won't meet my eyes.
Get back the way you were.
Where do you want it.
oh come on, just do it
Where
please
Please what.
please, you know
Ask nice.
Say pretty please with sugar on top.
pretty please with sugar on top
this is so stupid
Where do you want it.
everywhere.
Tell me everywhere forever.
forget it. i don't want to do it anymore.
Tell me forever.
forever
You don't mean it.
i mean it
You'll leave me.
i won't
Yes you will. You already have.
i'm trying.
Are you dying for me.

i'm dying for you.
No, really, would you die for me.
ummm
Tell me you'd die for me.
i'd die for you.
Say it like you mean it.
i would die for you.
I am dying for you.
I take my finger out of her ass.
I clamp her to me: nipple to nipple,clit to clit, slow, tight.
Then I fuck her in the cunt with my12" barrel.
I stick the handle up my cunt.
It hurts, shapes my cunt into a tight fist.
I fuck her hard.
I arch my back, stretch our long nipplesthin, pull our clits
closer and closer and closer.
stop. it hurts too much.
Too bad. You said you'd die for me.
I unclamp her clit.
Here.
I clamp my clit to her thumb, clit to thumb.
Hurt me.
She opens her eyes.
OK. she whispers. Jerk it!
I jerk up and down against her cunt metal dumb thumb
ripping my clit apart.
Hard, Harder, Hard, Harder, Harder. She makes low,
gutteral, cruel repetitions.
She watches my eyes. Dead cunt queenie eyes.
She doesn't love me anymore.
I express myself all over her cunt in clear sad ejaculations.
Waterfalls and waterfalls.
The barrel slips out.
no!
you stopped! why'd you stop!
She turns all sullen and won't come.
So roll over.
no.
Roll over bitch.
No!
I push her knees back and splay her butt.
So take it in the ass. Dry. Fucking cunt.
She whimpers but she doesn't mean it.
If she won't come in the cunt, she'll always come in the
ass.
You can give it, you can take it.
When I get it past the sphincter she stops fighting.
Cunt to dead ass.

We are connected now.

Basically I rape her in the ass with the barrel of my gun, handle shoved up my cunt so I can come too. Again and again and again and again.

Push out.

Suck it in.

I rape her because she's given up. She's not even using the power I gave her, clit clamp and all she could control me with and doesn't.

I push in the barrel when she tries to push me out.

Work with me.

It's hard keeping the handle in the right place when I quicken things.

It looks easier than it is.

She is screaming.

Fuck you.

I push my fist down her throat.

She pulls my clamps til I bleed.

O.K. O.K. I pop my hand out.

She vomits a nice thin green stream.

Nice. Choke on it.

She's passive now and begging.

I want to have a baby.

She has to go to the bathroom.

So go.

She tries to get up.

Don't move.

It'll hurt you more if you move.

I soften up, whisper in her ear

SSSssss

Pusssssh

ssssssssssssssss

She cries softly.

Relax hon.

Just relax.

I'll be gentle.

I put my finger in her ass.

push out

push.

like you're having a bowel movement

i can't

you can.

She whimpers.

let me go

She's totally given up.

No.

I fuck her tenderly in the ass until she start to lose control

Let go.

Come on hon let go of it.
Then I fuck her hard.
I love you.
She cries.
stop. it hurts too much.
Let go of it.
I love you.
She comes and fills the barrel of my gun.
I love you.
You smell like shit.
I push it in so hard my lips tighten around the trigger.
I could shoot her up here shoot her up the ass and end it all
while she's coming out shit globs all over my cunt hair. Shoot
her here before she leaves me. Shoot you up the ass cunt.
Fucking shoot you up the fucking dead ass cunt queenie you
you up the ass cunt. Shoot Dead ass cunt. Who have you got
to fuck you now. Who fucks a dead cunt? Shoot a Gun up your
asscunt Say you like it it your dead asscunt. Say you like it
fucking metal rod up your back cunt gun up your asshole.
Tell him. Tell him what you like.
So go ahead.
Go ahead shoot.
It's the 4th of July.

occupy the point at which a line and a column meet:
gender, race: not the place but the *rank:* the place one occupies
in a classification: dominator or dominated.

In short: The primary condition is total submission

I understand, and am all obedience.

I do not know the woman I am until I am raped.

I do not know the man I am until I rape.
You are a servo-user caught up in a power situation of which
you yourself are the bearer.

rape   raped
he "cells", "places", "ranks" your body parts

how to arrange:

the grid, the economic table, narrative, topolo-
gies, taxonomy, prisons, body organs, hospitals, boundaries,
Euclidean geometry, borderlines and borderlines, the move

ment of wealth, immigration and chain gangs, immigration
and the appropriation of bodies, immigration, migration, the
docility-utility relation, master it, bodies piled high on the
pavement, the spatial arrangement of men and women, chained,
bodies, the real furniture, splayed, real, but also ideal, because we are bodies projected on to this segmentary machine—
grid and plot, plot and grid, plot and pavement, plot and the
prevention of civil disorder, assessments and plots, discipline
and plots plots and plots and power and plots and corpses
handled piled on our TVs.
    I chain her wrists. Then I chain her ankles. Then I chain
her neck.

  • Leashes

  Circle fifth

        We're in the grocery store trying on dog leashes
            when the meat man goes by with a metal tray of
coiled sausages.

  • Windows

Unverifiable: Circle sixth   You never know whether you
are being looked at at any one moment; but you are always sure
that you may be so . . .

And so you are made PowerVisible (the most powerful Windows
surround you): You constantly have before your eyes the tall out-
line of the central observation tower: 19thcTEMPL.PANOPtic on I
am in and from which you are spied upon.
                        it is a crumbling struc
                        ture. Please wear a
                        hard hat.

            You are a prisoner in my viral novel now.
            You and Him and queenie too.

            I insert you in this fixed place behind my
powerful
Windows: Suddenly you see that you are a deer in my
scope!

                You cannot see even my shadow.

            I move inside you not though doors but through

Windows: zig-zag openings in the glass partitions that
intersect   the hall at right angles.

Windows: I insert a FlexCam

It's a great new tool

Flexcam's 60" swivel head and 18" flexible gooseneck offers
precise camera positioning—easily, quickly, flexibly.

Windows: the walls of her intestine appear
i have tack-sharp focus from a quarter inch to infinity.

It's plug in and use!

And the single-line cable carries all audio, video and power to
reduce desktop clutter.

Supports VideoSpigot, VideoBlaster, QuickTime or any other
Windows compatible video digitzer

It's remarkably easy!

            I insert into you your place, your body, your Win-
dows: disease, your death, your well-being.

            And then are you then the other--unformed as I
form you.
            Your slightest movements are supervised.

Windows: Just click and move and just one move and
CLICK!   you're done.

Windows: Do you suppose that you have left this world?
              The train leaves, arrives, leaves, the engine
              sputters, a telephone is ringing & ringing &
              ringing.

              AS YOU ARE MADE,

the telephone rings, the taperecorder says: Say something other than   tape recorder, something other
than tape recorder,   other than tape recorder

            television, video, computer, narrative, network,
structure, the 19th Century, the 20th Century,

YOU ARE UNMADE

VOI.RS in the GRID

circle seventh

The voice of the woman behind blue glass:

"Transportation you could say is merely a question of
another room gently."
It is more a white cell than a room really there are no
bars but an iron grid on the window as if outside could be so
contained as she could be inside.
"I am this. I am that."
She sits dangling her feet, on the edge of the bed.
"I have fifty years. I have sixty years."
She holds something in her hand.
"Here are knives and forks, relics of myself."
She carves a few windows in her skin.
"I am already eighteen and slicing."
The result is clear practice for, juice and no yellow stain.

Windows

☐Are you still jumping out of_____ in expensive hotels?

TO STOP: press ESC key.

enter ...
_____

TEMPL.ateAcceSS.F.:TEMPL.eMACRO.ME.NU:
TEMPL.ASSFs

_____

select one

☐smoothspace(ss), queenie, is where we can continue: circle
eighth

　　　　　　　　think of a long thing
　　　　　　　　does it have to be long to continue.
　　　　　　　　think of how i uncoil your colon
　　　　　　　　that's a long thing.

smoothspace(sssssss)
bend over girl
suck it up inside you
i hold the nozzle to her asshole
i clean her upper colon
i remove the whole hose
    then i insert a leaf, windscape (don't blow up me, you can't blow up a girl), an ocean still, a large boat in between her legs, my hand and my voice on the wooden railing i arrive i keep arriving and arriving by train she leaves behind a boat a

Transportation. . . is merely
another room gently

leaf a blaze of red, foliage, it is fàll. Transportation, and a boat to, abnormal sensations in the lower belly (it's from being butt-fucked), something, revolves, in the upper Mojave, (i like that picture a lot—it's so ordered, i say. she of course disagrees with me it's yours. i give it to her), sand, a boat, a grey dented rowboat, dryfucked, dead ass cunt spread on the map my wheels my wheels my wheels my wheels these are my wheels, what happened to my wheels, something knifelike. reconfirms her: I DO NOT KNOW THE WOMAN I AM UNTIL I AM RAPED.
A WOMAN
I AM RAPED

Am.i still

at GUNPOINT
i question her gender,
pull down your underwear
boy's race what color is your
in the back only
can you any gender fuck up the white ass.
bend over rent boy meets rent boy
open her anus and look!
butt-fucked up both a billy-club
and a dick
is she any woman there?
black shit on the station floor
there's a little spot of red and a big fat vein.
wipe it up
she looks pretty good for her age
first they make her eat some
she should dye her hair though
then they shave his balls
then they shove a billy-club
up his ass
I shave her here
then they wire him to
OK Little Red Leaf
here is where I shave you
Ha. Ha. There's no conflict between us now!
i shave her then i rape her
so you'll never rape again
O.K. here is where I fuck you
so bend over CUNT
Here is where I fuck and fuck you again & again & again.
She takes it because she has to. She's stuck in
He takes it because he has to. He's stuck in: first he raped me then he saved me.

Pose.
Not like that.
No.
No.
No.
Show me your asshole.

i masturbate while i watch her.
i masterbate while i watch him.

damage, damage, and postcards

dear 9,
   it's not you

dear 9.
   remember pearls?

   others follow.
   i press one in.
   i pull one out.

dear 9.
   how's your dead cunt.

   no fucking way.
   not in the ass.

   not that.

/./././././././.././././././././.sutur/././././././.././././././././.e
circle ninth

*JUST LET ME JUST LET ME JUST LET ME BE AND BE
AND BE PINK AND PINK METALLIC!*

ED: Yes, Weekly

   Just let me be and be the body electronic a pink to
sing to

   I just love to
   sing
   this
   song
   this
   song

metal and smooth space in between just let me be and be be the pink electronic body suit all metal and sky was all am-ethyst and the sky was all violence just to glitter and blow up you can't blow up a girl why not glitter and blow up your organ.on queenie you and me let's be petroglyphs across the sky why not forever xerox in our amethyst pink metallic body suit and sky you and me spread without organs our electronic body still electric you should learn to run without organs that have already exploded and now are all glitter, glitterati and shrapnel queenie an i.van i run with batteries now instead of organs i am the nomadic she novel disorganized lesbian no-mad traveling faster than my exgendered organs organs could let you fly behind me see them flapping in the breeze behind me you you you you're behind me now queenie mine is i.van i.van i am am.i forever my freeway van beyond you pink metal body suit cunt and sky all three stars are like little fishies all three stars are little fishies see them wriggle in the sky who needs you

Dear Narrator,

novel me the latest post-, please. Can you please make make me post-post and the latest post-cyber, post-female, post-post superhero and so described in writing across my pink metallic chest:

POST-LESBIAN NOMAD
TRAPPED IN A MAN'S BODY

q.
(i take my finger
out of her asshole.)

AMI: I don't know who or what or where I am anymore.

SU: Contact the International Narrative Society.

INS: Consider the natural: EXIT 13A.

> *EXIT13A: jungle,*
> *nature, loss,*
> *a NATural little*
> *narrative to*
> *next to sad*
> *sad   (abandon*
> *her*
> *exit 13B)*

TEMPL.emicroME.NU: (MACRO.ME.NU.NATural)

(select one:)

☐ plot plot & plot IN _____;

☐ novel by_____;

☐ RobE.rtRED.ford in _____;

☐ MURDER.ousVEG.etable.OR.GAN on_____;

☐ restorative vegetable growth of _____;

☐ the scent of frangipani blossoms in_____; &

☐ we're one step away from <u>CHAOS</u> theory.

WORDTRANS:
Open, pounding.

I hear them—women, say something!

> BWOOOO-WOOOO-WITT-WITT-WITT
> BWOOOOo BWOOOOO BWOOOO BWOOOO

☐ FEMALEHUMANHORNS: FEMINTERNEsTS;

FEMVIRalDIAlo gue(FEMVIRDIA)]

❑ The near and far, and the extreme
                        or vacuum range
                        bwoo bwwo
                        oowb oowb

TEMPLemacroMenu: PETROGLYPHS&CLIFFsGRRRRRLS

Get serious GLYPH.GIRLS:

It's back to petroglyphs & cliffs.

        spontaneous remission   what the body already
            knows is.

                        what mainstream america is reading
                        at the moment.
                                        (i write it all
                                        the TI.ME.)

            somehow NATure directs all this information
            in my direction. "My body is just the place my
            memories call HO.HO.HO.ME for the TI.ME being."

(we do not know the larger picture)   who is this sw.ami.
                                        the quantum alter
                        pen   na(rr)ator.
                        pene   trator
                                oh hi Ivan
            "i don't have picnic deficiency"

            "in my total defenselessness is my total invincibil-
ity."

                I am
                Φam   O am.I?
                fully present?   the illusion of chaos
                                    is my extended body
                                    for you WRI.Ders to know for
                                    your 120 to 130 years
                                    you don't begin middle age
                                    until 65

you are in the prime of your
life   SO GO
get serious glyph girls

E (X) = the expected value of X
change the expected value and you change the
reality

YOU ARE THE INTERPRETER. GET IT? THE BODY IS A
PRINTOUT.
CHA
YOU'RE THE INTERPRETER.
CHA
CHANGE THE PROGRAM.
CHA
YOU ARE THE PROGRAMMER.
CHA

"The self is in the silent space (s ss) between thoughts,
the windows to the cosmos."
s ss   sss

CHA

Back to meditation.
CHA
CHA

I GOT A GUN
I GOT A CUNT GUN
CHA   CHA CHA

inner stress which basically is the cause of all . . . let
go of your need for predictability & you're free. a
subtle shift of consciousness

I finally started functioning when I realized I
was God!
CHA!
WE ARE NOT THE EXPERIENCE WE III I IDENTIFY
SO MUCH W/ THE EXPERIENCE   CHA CHA
CHHH CCHHH   A   CHA NGE CH CH CH CHANGE ES
CHA   NGE   change the attn from the EXP to
thank you the EXPer & you (it can happen in an
Dr.   instant)) . . .
Deprok   A member of Friends of New Dimensions.
Chockra
mind body   Program #2391

medicine   (insert   space   memory
music)
ageless
body TI.ME   The institute of poetic science
less MIND.   Other New Dims. Radar Programs
                              Dept. K
                          Box 4100510
                            LA   CA

Chapter WHY: HOW.NATural

□   an age of brain growth . . .

....

Wash her naked organic body clean of civilization—body,
dirt, trash, and rot have been organized into information
between her parallel legs and time zones she is screened off
and

insert   space   memory   music

erased from the perfect world of her electronic body. And green!

"The trip has made me hungry, hungry."

Her electronic body looks so real and dry and wet. It moves around, gazes back, it communicates.

"Once I was privatized . . ."

I offer her go-get, bring-back, import-export, glycerine, buy-sell, flow and circuit, in suppository form and matter up her ass, crack, and drip ass cunt.

I fuck her anal hole, beauty, health, intelligence, cultural artifacts.

She accepts this enema tip.

I kept looking back as if i had forgotten something.

Outside it is snowing.

i miss you little glycerine

shut up

I fuck her with a wrench dry and wet. I fist fuck her colon. It takes a long time to get it up inside her.

She acquieses to the pain, says, "I hurt myself today."

"You hurt yourself good, queenie, have another needleful."

I rip the corners of her mouth when I ejaculate in her ass cunt I insert a metallic line, bite it, and watch her tear, swallow it, I feel her resistance grow and grow stronger and stronger it passes through her, I tug and tug it out her anus, a string of dead fishies, heart, kidney, liver, spleen, bowel, bowel coils and coils of bowel. I squeeze her bowel inch by inch to see what she will give me.

"Who are you."

"Just the opposite. Turn around."

I tug at a fish line hanging from her cunt. Out pops her

cervix. I dangle it. Dead fish. And drop it.

"Time slips, honey."

I tie the anal wire around my wrist.

"Hold on to it and walk."

"Fuck you."

I slap her on the liver. It jiggles and bleeds between her thighs.

"WALK, BITCH!"

She tries to walk away.

"Fuck you."

"Yeah, whatever."

She looks more femme now than ever. I drape a knotted strand of colon around her neck.

"Outside thought is not possible."

There is the sound of a snowplow scratching and scraping against the pavement.

"Ice or BE, MeatLoaf."

She has a carving knife.

My Beatrice.

"I do this only because I love you."

I follow her into the kitchen stuffing her organs back in, sheeplike.

The reciprocal implications: we face each other consuming, assimilating, excreting a whole hierarchy, the whole necessity of not having control over one's own body, data organs, weather, precipitates, excretions, one's own viral intoxicants, body fluids, street lamps, we are objects brought together no matter how far apart our contexts may be, a relationship is formed, language, wired, thin, thick, twisted delimits this body. We like our cats make low gutteral sounds.

Then:

☐ I remind a lot of people of frangipangi blossoms.

Then:

☐   the world grows hard again.

                            ICE OR BE
                            BEATRICe   (password)

                                                ___)

                            (: she was a
                            whore before)

Chapter 1: Once upon a time

   Another wave breaking. They wear green ribbons. Black
silver foam is unarranging in a beautiful clean tone.
   I said, That flute was like the autumn wind.
   It doesn't matter what I say.
   You're oddly magnetic to the death of things tonight.

   Death in a red hat death in I want to fall in love tonight.
Death in surpassing death death of entirely again and again
death in not supposing death, death a colored loss of ribbons
death of all singular death in a red sad sad curl death of a very
small pink cake death of red jell-o death in a large red box
death of any thunder death of twenty-four death in a red um-
brella death of every current organization death of dark red
death of dark cherry red death in a little green death of stable
temperature death death of a red horse death of white and
cream death in a light blue   stop

   a hole is a little red leaf death in between teeth death of a
center place bite death in a whole piece of toast with strawberry
jam death of a sudden suddenly death in different colors death of
a whole body hanging death in a little pink polka dot death in
between
   did you think of death in venice
   yes I did I thought of death in venice death in venice
california 6:03 am saturday february 13, 1993 practically a
sound reason to walk into the great abstact
   "I want to fall in love tonight."

   A woman leans both hands on the railing facing south.

I want to bend her over and over and soak her face in the Great Below. She is of course a dyke.

"The language that I spoke what was it."
It was the language that you spoke in the last century.
What was I in the last century.
You were stiff leaves burnt paper. You are also a girl, here in this room.
Make me lie. Make me crouch. Make me sweep my hair all in one curve.
You must love me very very much.

A woman leans both hands on the railing facing south.
I want to touch her but she is all back behind blue glass.

A woman leans her hands on the railing facing south.
"Red Leaf. Red Leaf," she calls ardently, inexhaustibly in every kind of weather startled by her own body's beautiful muscular sobs, round with body hair glistening.
The tears she shed will surely overwhelm the land and leave it a faceless ocean. This is an old sentence.

After thirty-two years she establishes her own land and builds a palace for herself. Everyone calls her Celestial Goddess of Fire and Thunder. Venomous Queen of the Celestial Essences. Of Fire. And Thunder.
Why are you still so angry?

Death of a very small pink cake

As long as you do the great rite of the Womb-Store Mandala you will live eighty-one years. Isn't that enough for you.

No.

A woman leans both hands on the railing facing south.
When she dies she leaves no body behind.
Her back was as red and wet as newly washed silk.
"I saw you here, alone at sea."
She answered with a smile.
And I wanted so much to talk to you.
I came on the cloud and winds.
Oh be kind and speak to me tenderly.
How could I not love you.
They reached a large island.
Her fragrant form, borne by the clouds and the wind, floated up and vanished into the blue sky.

She rushed home in a rage, shut herself up in silence in her room, and quickly died.

And with these words they flew up into the sky.

TEMPLmacroMENU: womenwarmachine!

Chapter __ : never in reverse

    3. Treasures from the Mutter Museum
    1. once upon a time, or
    2. The existing structures do not work for me
....

Chapter 2. The existing structures do not work for me

On every side you perceive the peril of the infrastructure taking on water, ranked, rippling, hanging from eleven nine-inch nails.

Your tongue, your stylus, and ten survivors are forced to find refuge the natural story: in caves, in huts made of palm fronds, or best of all, in the branches of tree houses.

I hold up my hand and say: *Listen, this is the true*

story of the woman who is raped. This situation of exchanging one neural memory for another.

Her.

Imagine her a splash of hyperred neon.

Imagine her something almost paradise about to begin:

EAT   *EAT*   *EAT*

it pulses and then spurts.

(it's hard for a girl when the blood won't come)

Imagine a very little red leaf and a medium-sized boat about to continue this novel little ocean scene anywhere still and green and a large wanting to ascend this suture and scene.

This and a blush of crimson on her boy's underwear.

Imagine this novel RE.LA.VIR anywhere there is a half an ocean cliff and half a pink, still, enlarged and sought for a very large scene and wish sought for a stable color not to be changed into any other kind of color arriving in between the now and climax not past mauve and sand or yet to come pink and fluid cliff *EAT NOW YOU KNOW HOW   NOW EAT* in the infinitive *TO EAT NOW NOW TO EAT NOW AND NOW* and swell in to now two or three and now you know and not history that's too tight a suture to but not to now eat and wider at the edge of a half a pink cliff in between a sudden RE.d LEAF and one thonged foot down down in and then up one thonged foot up and up and half a pink climb and a wave already gone wave and RE.d Identified.

– –

TEMPLME.NU: WATER, PINK CAKE, AND GLYPH

☐ DINNERCONVERSATION

Good-bye.

Good-bye *Clinamen* and mint.

Did you eat already?

Yes I ate. I ate you. I ate you YOU. I HATE YOU and all your explications. Haven't I said this all before a million times.

Is there anything else to say?

What I miss is all the lovely patter.

We wave to her I I identified I-Disneyfied I-petroglyphed and I-past now.

Good-bye

❑ Love, Discharge, and You

One may watch what I do to my material self watch what I write I write when I squeeze off my body organs and insert plastic and metal expansion boards. Then I become all electronic—disturbance, discharge discharge, and goo.

Yucky goo.

Oh ick.

I always find viscosity so erotic, don't you?

I always carry a spray can of WD-40.

I carry one in the front pocket of my jeans so I look like a guy with a big dick. It's not that.

I keep the other in my drawer with my sex toys.

I don't have a lover, but I masturbate twice a day.

I like to do it to myself in the ass, but it makes a big mess.

Every kind of goo turns me on.

Like now, just writing this. My pussy's all tingly and I'm thinking about what I could do to a woman's asshole. Sometimes I want to tear the corners of her mouth and make her cry while I watch her face and mine in the mirror.

I want to fuck her like a dog, and so I saddle the maximum hardware and I am very pleasantly occupied for an hour.

Who is she—

☐ cunt or cunt to.

I saw you again, he said, in the window last night you were shaving with a woman I saw every move of the razor she held you didn't dare to move did you when she lay you on the bed you let her shave your nipples and then you let her shave your cunt and then your asshole.

He slips into her upreared.

That page you were reading. I didn't know it was in there til now, what did you insert.

It's as if her body were the wallpaper. (Or as if her body were this:)

A scene where her nipples point, flare, spurt blood. He encourages this—with his mashed potatoes.

[INSERT]: writing in the dark

whereas in reading, he slips a piece of paper up inside her eye, glides it along more smoothly some irregular line like this:

***Draw this irregular line

stall (what's that got to do w/E.EPISTOL)
    it's the nature of plot

NEOplastic   NODE or NEOplastic
                  NODES
1. I DO NOT KNOW THE WOMAN I
                  AM
2. I DO NOT KNOW THE WOMAN I neroli oil   a pale yellow
                  AM essential
3. I DO NOT KNOW THE WOMAN I   obtained from
                  AM orange flowers
4. I DO NOT KNOW THE WOMAN I
                  AM repo : REPURCHASE AGREEMENT
5.   UNTIL

6. I DO NOT KNOW THE WOMAN I   my guess is she was raped

```
                        AM
7.                      UNTIL   SHUT UP REPLEADER
8. I DO NOT KNOW THE WOMAN I
                        AM   replicon
9.                      UNTIL
10. I DO NOT KNOW THE WOMAN I  replicative <the __ form
of
                        AM  tobacco
11.                     UNTIL
12.             I AM RAPED         mosaic virus>
```

replicon   [replicate + ^{2}-on] (1963) :   a linear or
    circular section of DNA or RNA which replicates
    sequentially as a unit

stall
stall

sarsaparilla

Sasquatch

^{1}sass
^{2}sass

savant

super
stupid
state capitalism
^{3}spurt
^{4}spurt
^{5}spurt
squirt
steamroller
steamroller
steamengine
^{1}staple
^{2}staple
^{3}staple
^{6}staple
^{1}stapler
^{2}stapler
^{3}stapler   (draw irregular line)
star

standstill

stalag

Stalinism
3stalk
stalk.ing_horse
1stall \n\ L *locus* place, Gk *stellein* to set up, place,
    send] (bef. 12c)
2stall *vt* (14c) . . . 3a : to bring to a standstill : BLOCK;
    esp: MIRE   b : to cause (an engine) to stop
    usu. inadvertently. __ *vi* 1 : to come to a
    standstill(as from mired wheels or engine failure)
3stall
4stall [n. alter. of *stale* (lure)](1914) : a ruse
    to deceive or delay
5stall
stall-feed
1stamp
2stamp
1stampede
2stampede *vb* stampeded; stampeding.

excuse. me
VANtheMANIfoldDYKE.

BEND THE FUCK OVER SISTER.

I GOT A CUNTGUN.

JUST RELAX JUST O TO SLEEP JUST RELAX JUST RELAX JUST O
TO SLEEP JUST RELAX JUST O TO SLEEP JUST RELAX JUST
RELAX JUST O TO SLEEP

i hope that you will not

        IV:

        queenie

        (the drug that cares more)

i'm really dumb stupid.

they found pieces of jennifer's

where is the

baby

i want my baby

there is no baby

body

                         ☐ ABOATABOUT

hope
7 5/16

i sure miss Zanzibar

9/ 32		under 123
etc. vert dist. = 1 3/16		under 1-2-3
		plastic bridge
small boat	headless boat	plastic bridge
		plastic bridge
	(resting on	plastic bridge
	wood of	plastic bridge
	plastic	plastic bridge
	bridge.)	plastic bridge
black boat	head of boat	plastic bridge
	long boat	
	boat	skip
	boat	one
rubber boat		short
rubber boat	lg.&long boat	boat
rubber boat	boat	
	boat	(Draper's
boat in thin		Bridge)
rubber casing		
		4 7/16
repeat		
plastic	plastic	
plastic	5X	over 17 7/16
plastic		
plastic		over2 17 13/16
plastic		over 17 29/32

```
        plastic                      under   18 3/32
      boat with                      over    18 9/32
        rubber
```

NARRTRANS=ON

NARRTRANS: *As I Crossed a Bridge of Dreams,*

TEMPLE.microME.NU

☐ Someday You Will Be Raped Like I Was Raped

☐ Someday You Will Rape Like I Rape

Writing in the dark

TEMPLmacroMENU: PETROGLYPHGRRRRRLs

....
Chapternomic: Jurassic

Record of the rocks . . .
....

        Hope:

      rubber boat   boat
                             boat   (Draper's
      boat in thin   Bridge)
      rubber casing
                                         4 7/16 repeat
      plastic   plastic
      plastic   5X   over   17 7/16
      plastic
      plastic   over2 17 13/16
      plastic   over   17 29/32
      plastic   under 18 3/32
      boat with   over   18 9/32
        rubber

NARRTRANS=ON   Strap it ON!

[NARRTRANS: Almost a thousand years ago a book with no
name was written by a

woman with no name.]

There was a woman who had once been an intimate friend.

Then she married the Governor of Echizen.

She accompanied him to his province in a boat after which I heard no more from her. I managed to send her this poem:

Good-bye

queenie
Apocolypse
Morphine
Show- and Tel-e-ol-o-gy
Linear Ornament, everyday life
intelligible, Moral ideology,
ARPAnet.

TRUTH AND LOVE SUCK.

Hello

VirtualCunt
Ice
Tools
Weapons
MetalSigns
Genital
Jewelry
AnalBeads
AbstractMachines
Sabbat
JiffyLube
AniLinctus
WD-40

SisterMachineGun

I live for your 12-inch dildo.

SIM4\RE.LA.VIR:
hope

hope, she has a head

Now, rebirth into the Land of Bliss is not unknown, but those who achieve it leave their bodies behind as a sign.
I really had reached Paradise in the flesh.
Paradise in the palm of my hand.

But I want to be born into Paradise,too.Why must I go back.
Because you have done nothing to deserve staying.
Then what can I do to be sure of Paradise.

Then shave my head.
It's wonderful to hear you say that but I can't do it all of a sudden.
How dare you come between me and Paradise. This morning as usual I was wanting more women but now as far as I'm concerned you can all get out and go wherever you please. I'm not keeping any of you.

She shed unrestrained tears of grief.
She had a little gong which she hung around her neck.

Now I'm going to go West. I'll keep calling Red Leaf Red Leaf and beating this gong until she answers.
She went off shouting, "Hey Red Leaf. Red Leaf. Hey. Hey."

She did just what she said she'd do: she went straight West calling "Red Leaf. Red Leaf. Hey. Red Leaf," and beating the gong.

Do you have anything else to eat.
Hey. Hey. Red Leaf. Where are you.
Here I am! replied an awesome voice from the depths of the sea.
Did you hear that?
Don't you want anything. I brought you some parched rice.

Will you trade your body for Paradise.
An equally constant stream leaving.

Letters from Paradise.

I desire rebirth into the Land of Bliss. Not that she was alone in the wish but she aspired so fiercely to Paradise that others' desire paled in comparison.
"Come to me before the day is over."
She would write.
On the last day of the year she would write on a piece of paper:"Come to me before the day is over. Do not fail!"
"Knock on the door. I'll ask who's there and you'll say 'A

messenger from _____ in the Land of Perfect Bliss, with a letter for you.'" Then she would go to bed.

At dawn the obedient acolyte would knock at the door of her hut.

Who's there.

A messenger from _____ in the Land of Perfect Bliss, with a letter for you.

The woman would stumble forth, weeping with joy. "What does it say," she would cry and reverently inspect the writing. Next she would collapse, overcome with deep emotion.

This happened every year.

The acolyte got quite good at the part.

This year I really believe _____ is coming for me, she declared, and I'll die!

Well, well, perhaps you will, who knows? She did not quite know what to say.

She seemed too overcome to move. Actually, though, she had just
died.

She was calling the Name one night when she heard a voice from the heavens saying "You have devoutly trusted me and have called my Name countless times. Early tomorrow afternoon, at the hour of the Sheep, I promise I will come and welcome you into my western Paradise. Do not stop calling upon me!"

When the time came, there was a gleam in the west. _____ appeared in glory like the full autumn moon breaking through the clouds, and the woman was bathed in the sublime rays that streamed from between her eyebrows. Flowers floated down from the sky. _____ advanced among downy purple clouds to offer her the lotus throne.

Here sit on it.

She mounted the throne and sailed away westward.

A week or so later, _____ decided it was time to make a bath and went into the mountains to cut firewood. When she came to a great cryptomeria growing over a waterfall she heard fowl cries from high up in the tree. A woman was there, tied naked to a branch. A particularly good climber, she discovered that it was _____who had sailed away to Paradise. She was tied to the tree with liana vines.

"_____. What happened?"

"She promised she'd be back for me any minute and she told me to stay right here. Don't you go untying me!"

XXXXXXXXXXXXXXXXXXXXXXXeofXXXXXXXXXXXXXXXXXXXXXXXXXX
XXXnoXXXXXXXXXXXXXXXXXXXXXXXXXXXXXXi'mXXXXXXXXXXXXX
notXXXXXXdoneXXXXXXXXXXyetXXXXXXXXXXXXXXXXXXXXXXXXXX
XXXXXXXXXXXXXXXXXrollXXXXXXXXXXXXXXXXoverXXXXXXXXXXXXX
XXXANDXXXXXXXXXXXDIEXXXXXXXXXXINXXXXXXXXXXXXXXXXXXXX
XXXXXXXXXXXXXXXXXXXXXLA.VIRNXXXXXXXXXXXXXXXXBITCHXXX
XXXX